FANG GANG 2

CYN

Dream - I can't believe it has almost been a year. Mommy loves you always. 🤍

CONTENTS

DARKNESS. It was all Fallon could sense as pain engulfed her. There was no light. There was no sound, nothing to touch, and nothing to see. She felt every last one of her blood cells bursting and then being put back together again, but what bothered her the most was the taste. Metallic and coppery… the taste of blood. It filled her mouth and stayed in the area between her throat and her lips. She craved it so badly she was sure she would go insane.

Time was lost to her, but even that didn't bother her because between the excruciating torture her body was going through and her thirst for blood, there was literally nothing else to think about. In the time her body was transforming, there were no thoughts of Kendrick or of the gang. She didn't fear death, nor did she think of her grandmother. School was not a factor, nor was the stranger named Remington who had put her in this predicament.

Five days she stayed like that, in a place where nothing but pain and a thirst for blood existed. Meanwhile, The Fang Gang made sure she was as comfortable as possible, setting her up in a guest room and waiting for her to wake up around the clock. The only reason she wasn't in her own bed was because Remington refused to watch over her in the room she and Kendrick had shared. At first, Kendrick didn't give a fuck what Remington wanted. In fact, he still didn't. The issue was that Kendrick found out pretty quickly what Remington's ability was, and that made it so there wasn't shit he could do about it. Best believe the two had fought as soon as they ensured Fallon was still breathing after the bite. Their parents let them duke it out and fuck The Lair up. The Gang even joined in when they saw how strong Remington was. Even with four vampires on one, Remington came out winning. Once he asserted his dominance, he let everyone know how shit was going to go. Even Prima and Maximus fell in line, which had never happened in the history of their vampirism.

Since then, Prima and Maximus had gone back to Jamaica, and the gang had all pretty much kept their distance from Remington unless it was their turn to sit with Fallon, who stayed under Remington's careful watch. Remington didn't leave the room with her in it once. He hadn't had human blood in days, but that wasn't shit to him. He would wait as long as it took for Fallon to wake up. Not even his cell phone distracted him from taking in every one of Fallon's features while he monitored the rise and fall of her chest. He knew the pain she was experiencing and the thirst that accompanied it, but he also knew Fallon was a fighter. She would be okay. He was confident in that.

Over the five days, Remington managed to form somewhat of a cordial relationship with Papa. The two would talk idly while Papa was checking in on Fallon. The ass-whooping Remington put on Papa when he jumped in his and Kendrick's fight was long forgotten, but Papa was careful, though. He may have realized Remington wasn't all bad just by conversing with him, but he was loyal to the gang, so he kept shit real cool. Not only was Scarlette loyal to the gang, she was loyal to her best friend, so she was conflicted. On one hand, she would find a way to kill Remington herself if Fallon somehow didn't come out of this okay. On the other hand, she was secretly happy someone got up the nerve to bite Fallon. It was no secret that Scarlette was a bit on the selfish side. She truly loved Fallon, and many times she thought about biting her best friend herself to see if she would turn. She didn't want there to come a day when Fallon was no longer with them. Since the two had become close, she dreaded that day and hoped Kendrick and her would decide to turn her. Remington swooped in and made that decision for everyone. She was happy as hell that Fallon had not died, and she seemed to be turning, but she wasn't so sure Fallon would be happy about the change. She would ride for Fallon no matter what, but she couldn't lie and say her heart didn't skip for joy every time she thought of an eternity with her bestie. Axel was not only loyal to the gang, but he was Kendrick's right hand. He also didn't appreciate anyone in the gang being challenged, let alone the entire gang. The fact that Remington had single-handedly took the gang down, and the fact that he could have ended all their lives if he had chosen to put Axel on edge. When it was his turn to sit with Fallon, since Kendrick didn't want Remington alone with her, he didn't have shit to say to Remington, even though Remington tried. Kendrick was another story. Remington didn't have shit to say to his brother, and Kendrick felt the same. The two had a millennia-long beef that Remington's sudden appearance had reignited in their lives.

To say The Lair was tense the past several days

was an understatement, but the question that was collectively on everyone's minds was when would Fallon wake up? Kendrick was becoming more and more worrisome as the days passed, and the gang was doing all they could to keep him calm. Remington, on the other hand, was as cool as a cucumber. He was a patient man, but he was slightly nervous about how Fallon would recieve him once she woke. There were things nobody understood, and he knew they would come to light sooner or later. The question that had plagued his mind was if Fallon would be able to help him tell his story, or if he would be left to explain it all on his own. He was also on guard because he knew once Fallon woke, things would be different. He knew his little brother had yet to face the fact that Fallon would now be his mate once she woke. It was true that not all mates were romantic, and he knew that was what Kendrick was hoping for, but Remington knew his brother's entire world was going to be shattered. Not that he truly cared, but he did have some decency left in his cold heart for his brother. Although Kendrick and his parents tried enslaving him to the cold for an eternity, he still had a sliver of loyalty to Kendrick, even if he didn't want to. Remington's goal wasn't to ruin his brother's life, despite what it may have seemed like. His goal was simply to take back what was his.

In a rare moment where Remington was alone with Fallon, he decided to sit on the bed next to her and hold her hand. He only did this on those rare times where they were alone. He wasn't a nigga that would outwardly showcase his feelings, and he didn't want the gang to know how deep his feelings ran for the sleeping beauty that had been causing all this fuss. He caressed her hand gently, a lump forming in his throat as he looked into her face while simultaneously listening for someone coming so he could resume his position in the chair in the corner of the room. All kinds of emotions ran through him. It had been a long ass time since he cried. His heart had turned cold centuries ago, but Fallon Bordeaux seemed to pull shit out of him that had been buried deep.

"Wake up, baby," he whispered so lowly there was no way anyone else in the house would be able to hear him, even with their sonic hearing. He was wrong, though. Someone had heard him. It was the first thing Fallon had heard in days. She squeezed his hand, and her brows knitted together in concentration. She heard Remington's plea, and everything in her wanted to oblige him, so a few seconds later, her eyes slowly opened and adjusted to the darkness. The window was closed with the blackout shades drawn. One quick look around the room told her that, but still, she could see every detail of the room clear as day, down to a speck of lint on the carpet that was several feet away and almost completely hidden. Her sight was inhumane as she looked around the room before her eyes landed on the man holding her hand.

Remington's heart picked up as he watched Fallon wake up and take in her surroundings. If he had known all he had to do was ask her to wake up, he would have done that days ago, but he should have known. It was how strong their bond was... how strong it had always been.

She peered at him with wide eyes, and tears immediately fell as she gasped. She reached her hand up to his face and caressed it lovingly. "Remy?"

Remington smiled for the first time in what felt like centuries. "It's me, my love."

Fallon closed her eyes and let her mind settle slightly before she opened them again and found Remington's curious eyes. She took a pained breath before saying, "I remember everything."

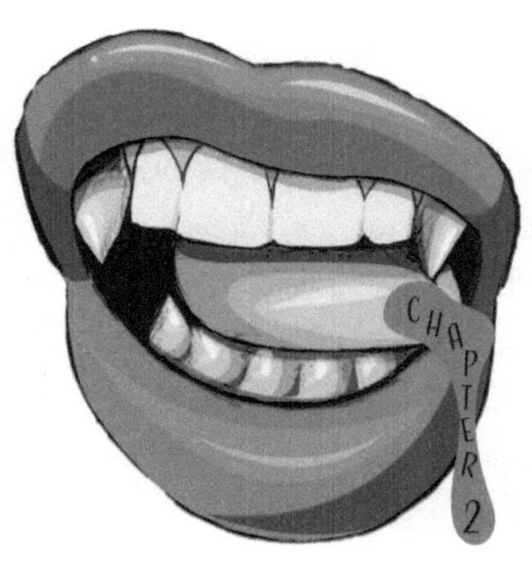

Over nine hundred years ago

FALLON RESTED *her head on Remington's shoulder as she drew lazy circles around his pecks. She raised her head and looked into his brown eyes, smiling sadly at him. "What art thee bethinking?"*

Remington gazed into Fallon's green eyes and caressed her cheek lovingly. She was the only woman he ever had the pleasure of being with, and she was the only woman he ever wanted to experience. His love for her was divine, but it was also forbidden, for her family were outcasts because they practiced witchcraft.

"I wisheth this couldst lasteth forever," he finally replied before he kissed her temple, her wild ginger curls

splaying out every which way. "I never wanteth to beest without thee, and I wanteth to openly loveth thee."

Fallon sighed deeply before raising from the pile of hay they'd been gallivanting on. Pieces of the fine straw stuck to her hair and sweaty body, but she paid it no mind as she reached for her discarded dress that lay on the ground next to the pig's pin. The dirty farmhouse they were in was not the most romantic, nor was it comfortable. The noises the animals made weren't a great soundtrack for love-making, but it was the best they could do. If anyone spotted them together, not only would Fallon be in danger for breaking the treaty with the townspeople, Remington would be exiled, or worse… burned at the stake right along with the love of his life. In order to be discreet, the farmhouse had turned into their little slice of heaven, no matter the smells it produced or how dirty it was. It was a price they each gladly paid.

Remington stood, naked as the day he was born, and grabbed the garment in Fallon's hands before pulling her into him, her back to his chest, their bodies still slick with the lovemaking that had just occurred.

"I didn't mean to maketh thee madeth," he said as he rubbed both his large hands up and down her arms, causing goosebumps to fill her body. Her nipples hardened, and her head fell back against his chest.

"I knoweth. I just wanteth thee out of harm's way," Fallon admitted, but Remington already knew that.

"I am in harm's way every second I am not with thee. Mine own heart can't taketh it any longer."

Tears welled in Fallon's eyes before she turned around and peered up at Remington with her emerald eyes. "Remy…"

"I knoweth," he replied somberly, with his head down. Remington knew Fallon's younger sister, whom she lived with, was starting to question her about where she was disappearing to, and Remington's family was asking similar questions. He knew it was only a matter of time before they were caught. Fallon felt the same things deep within her gut. Being a witch, a powerful one, at that, gave her a great sense of intuition, and it was why she had been cherishing every moment she had with Remington, because she was unsure how many more they would get. It broke her heart that a love as pure as theirs was so hard to settle in, but that was the hand they were dealt.

"Beest not," Fallon replied, as she chewed on her lower lip while knitting her brow.

Her mind kept skirting dangerous territory over the past several months, and this conversation with Remington was not helping one bit. Remington saw the conflict in her eyes and asked, "What is it?"

Fallon reluctantly lifted her eyes to him, contemplating if she should put the idea that had been plaguing her mind out into the universe. She knew once she did, there was no taking it back. Holding secrets from her love wasn't some-

thing she was used to doing, even if this wasn't a secret, per say. It was only an inkling of a thought she had yet to breathe life into. Still, she opened her mouth to respond. "What if it be true I findeth a way for us to beest together for an eternity?"

"How? Can thee doth that?" he asked, hope surging through him. Fallon was a powerful witch, that much he knew. He'd seen her cast spells beyond imagination. Not even her sister, Lily, could achieve her level of witchcraft, but he doubted she would be able to do as she just suggested.

"I'll findeth a way, dear Remy," she replied earnestly. "Art mine own powers not of the most high?"

"Of course, my dear… but —"

"Nay. I wilt findeth a way," she replied, now sure of herself. Losing Remington Danger was not something she ever wanted to experience. Speaking the nagging thought that had been plaguing her and putting it out into the universe sealed the deal for her. Fallon had always been careful with her words. She knew they held power, much like her bloodline. Staring into Remington's eyes now caused her to see what needed to be done. At that moment, she manifested something more powerful than she even understood. She stood on her toes and kissed his lips before grasping her frock once again and getting dressed. "Meeteth backeth here in a week's timeth."

Before Remington could respond, Fallon was leaving

the farmhouse, leaving him naked, confused, and hopeful for his future.

Fallon paced the length of the farm house nervously, hoping Remington showed. She had been pacing for an hour, and her nerves were getting the best of her. She had barely slept over the past week, and exhaustion grasped at her, but she knew she needed to fight on a little longer so she could see her destiny through. She'd had an intuition that the potion would work, and the thrill that overcame her was astounding. She was so close to having the life she deserved with the man she loved. First, he just needed to show his face.

Finally, he did. He snuck into the dark farmhouse, as the sun had fallen, leaving only the moon casting light. When his eyes adjusted and landed on Fallon, he smiled before rushing over to her. "I'm sorry for keeping thee waiting. Kendrick and Audrey did stay up late."

"Nevermind," Fallon spoke, waving him off before pulling the potion she'd been working on over the past week out of the pocket of her frock. It was wrapped in sheepskin carefully so it didn't spill. "I did it."

"What is it?" Remington asked, as he eyed the potion in Fallon's hands.

"'Tis the answer to all our problems. Our eternity, my love."

Remington's eyes sparkled before he grabbed for the potion to get a better look at the thing that would grant him his deepest desires. Fallon pulled away, though, and sat on a nearby haystack. "There art conditions thee may not concur to."

"I shall concur to anything to beest with thee for an eternity," Remington replied, sitting beside her and taking her hands.

Fallon shook her head. Although she had an intuition about the potion being a success, she still wasn't sure how he would take what she was about to tell him. "Listen, my love." Remington's smile fell from his face, and he settled down enough to listen to what Fallon had to say. She nodded when she noted his undivided attention before continuing. "This potion shall turneth us into something different. We shall not beest the same. Stronger, so we doth not to adhere to humans. Faster, so we can outrun any angry mob. There may beest side effects that art unforeseen. But we shall liveth forever with only one condition. To keepeth our strength and agility about us, we has't to feedeth on human blood."

Remington pulled away slightly. "Human blood? Why?"

Fallon's eyes turned to the ground. "An eternity is a longeth timeth. I could not risketh the binding being something that may not beest in ten thousand years. People shalt always beest, nay?"

"What about water? Dirt? Could there be nothing else?" Remington asked. "What if it be true humans befall the earth?"

Fallon shook her head. "Water and dirt did not has't the right properties. I hath tried everything. Mine owneth blood was the only thing that did complete the potion. I hath tried mine own sister's blood just to beest certain, and it worked a second timeth. Human blood wast the only thing that would bindeth us to an eternity. As longeth as humans existeth, we shalt, too."

An eternity with Fallon was what he wanted. Being stronger and faster were bonuses. A little human blood here and there was a price he was willing to pay, but in order to be certain of what he was getting himself into, he had one question to ask, "How much human blood?"

Fallon shrugged. "I wisheth I kneweth. I only knoweth 'twill becometh liketh our food. How often or how much I doth not knoweth."

"Shall we hast to kill?" he asked reluctantly.

Once again, Fallon shrugged. "I knoweth not."

Remington stood and paced the farmhouse, much like Fallon had only moments prior. Killing was not in his blood. He never thought he would have to kill anyone. He glanced at Fallon, who looked at him with tear-filled eyes. This moment was monumental, that much he knew. He understood her emotions. His response would change their lives forever, and how could he deny them the path they both so desperately wanted? At that moment, for once in his life, he decided to be selfish. As the oldest of three kids, he often found himself doing for others and doing as others pleased. Very rarely did he do something for himself. If it meant harming others to get what he wanted, then so be it. He hoped it didn't come to that, but he would do whatever he could to be with Fallon, and the most important part was they would do it together. He sat back down and said, "I wanteth to doth it."

Fallon knew he would. She had a week to mull over the contingencies of the potion, and she knew she was asking a lot of Remington to make his decision within minutes, but the longer they waited, there was more of a chance of them getting caught. Both their nerves had been increasing surrounding their relationship, and Fallon knew her intuition was always spot on. It was now or never, for she feared if they passed up this opportunity now, there wouldn't be another.

"Art thee sure?" she asked, wanting to be entirely sure before they went through with the process.

Remington nodded eagerly, not wanting to think too much about how this would impact him. All he could think of was his love for Fallon. The tears she had been holding in welled over as she pulled out a second sheep skin, handing it to Remington.

He grasped it before carefully unfolding it and gazing at the blood red liquid. He looked up at Fallon and asked, "What doth thee calleth this?"

Fallon's green eyes glinted in the moon. "Vampirism."

Present Day

FALLON CLUTCHED REMINGTON'S hands as flashes from her previous lives filtered through her mind. One thing that was always true about witches was they were reborn every few lifetimes. Each witch could remember her previous lifetimes as early as two years old, and they were always re-born within their own bloodline, making their magic stronger with each generation. It was why the Bordeaux family were the strongest. Their witches dated back several millennia, and no other bloodline could compare. In this lifetime, however, Fallon had not remembered that she was a witch, nor had she been born with magic. It had also been centuries since she had been reborn. Her brows furrowed in confusion. "What happened—"

The door swung open, and Kendrick rushed in followed by the rest of the gang, cutting Fallon off. Kendrick damn near knocked Remington out of the way to get to Fallon, and Remington let him. Now that he knew Fallon remembered, he was at ease. Whatever connection she and his brother had previously, that shit was dead now, and he smirked slightly as he stood and gave them some room, never taking his eyes off the love of his life.

"You're awake," Kendrick whispered as he hugged Fallon to his chest.

She stiffened slightly as she peered over at Remington over Kendrick's shoulder as guilt filled her. She had only been awake for about a minute, but she hadn't thought about Kendrick once. In fact, she had forgotten entirely about him.

When Fallon saw that Remington had a slight smirk on his face and was hanging back without a care in the world, she relaxed. Suddenly, her priorities had shifted, and Remington's feelings were at the top of her list. So much was happening in the span of a couple of minutes, and her head was spinning. The pointy fangs her tongue kept finding its way toward wasn't lost on her, either. She was just doing her best to ignore them for the time being, even though the thirst she felt was unbearable. Becoming a vampire was never anything she wanted… in this life, at least. Her mind was going haywire with memories and fresh knowledge of who she really was. Kendrick hugging her was acting as an unwanted distraction, and at that thought, she cringed because she felt bad for thinking that way.

When he pulled back and stared into her eyes, she saw so much love, and that shit had her in a chokehold… and not in a good way. Fallon now remembered how consuming her love had been for Remington, and it was sad, but those feelings overrode the feelings she had for Kendrick. It was like there was a sudden shift within her. Remington was now her… she didn't even know what he was to her now, and she knew a conversation needed to be had to sort it all out, but Kendrick… her feelings for Kendrick were very clear. There were no romantic ones. It was odd, but she now looked at him more like a friend. She was even inclined to feel a sisterly bond with Kendrick, but she immediately pushed those feelings aside. It made sense, if she thought about it. Her and Kendrick had been fated to be brother and sister in law a millennia ago, but seeing as she fucked that man every which way… she couldn't think of him as a brother. No matter what happened. That didn't change the fact that she very much still only thought of him as a friend. The love he was pouring into her through this hug was definitely reciprocated. She still loved Kendrick dearly, but not in that way.

She cleared her throat and finally whispered, "Hey."

Kendrick's smile faltered, and he didn't miss Fallon's eyes shifting to Remington, who stood behind him. The way his heart shattered was palpable. Everyone in the room could feel the shift in Kendrick's energy as he realized his worst nightmare was coming true right before his eyes.

"Man… fuck no," he whispered, and then louder he said, "You don't love that nigga, Fallon. The mating bond isn't romantic. You don't know him like I do, baby. You—"

"Kendrick…" Fallon whispered, a lone tear falling down her cheek. She had never seen him look so broken. He was the leader of The Fang Gang. He was strong with a gang of savages beside him, but the way he was looking now made Fallon second guess everything she thought she knew about him. It was then she realized she was Kendrick's one and only weakness. She knew his love for her was bigger than she could have ever imagined, and not too long ago, she would have shared the same sentiment, but looking at him now, it all became clear to her.

Kendrick was consumed by her. She feared it was too much like the way she was consumed with Remington. Even now, as she watched Kendrick break right before her, the green eyes that were now bloodshot due to the untamable thirst within her, shot over to Remington. She was in awe that he was here. The fact that it took this long to reunite them was unbelievable to her. She wanted to run to him, to talk to him, to take him in… but Kendrick needed her. Her heart was torn, and Remington could sense this was all too much for her.

He stepped forward and placed his hand gently on Kendrick's shoulder. For her sake, he would play nice. "Ken—"

It happened so fast. Fallon was sure had she still been human, she would have missed it, but her eyes and mind were able to register Kendrick standing up and delivering an uppercut to Remington's chin. Remington flew back and hit the wall opposite the bed. Fallon didn't remember telling her body to move, but one second she was in bed, and the next she was at Remington's side, just as he landed on his feet in a fighting stance. The niggas were really trying to square up at a time like this. Fallon understood that emotions were high… but nah. This wasn't it.

"Cut it the fuck out!" she shrieked.

Both men ignored her as they mugged each other.

Kendrick was the first to speak. "You've taken everything from me, nigga. You just had to come and take my girl, too?"

Remington scoffed. "I took everything from you? Nigga, I *gave* you everything. This gang of yours… it wouldn't exist if it wasn't for me. Nigga, *you* wouldn't exist if it wasn't for me."

Fallon's eyes grew wide as realization hit her. Of course Remington was responsible for Kendrick being a vampire. That meant their parents were also the result of Remington biting them. Her head felt like it literally exploded as she thought about what she had created. She wondered why the two brothers were at odds. She had so many questions, and apparently, so did the gang.

"Can someone tell us what the fuck is going on here?" Papa asked as he looked at the three vampires caught up in a budding love triangle.

"This nigga has no heart. He's dangerous, and he's supposed to be fuckin' dead, and now, Fallon is mated to him… romantically," Kendrick spat.

"Kendrick, it's so much more than that—"

"You don't know what the fuck you're talking about!" Fallon was cut off by Kendrick's outburst.

Fallon looked at him with sad eyes. "I know more than you think," she whispered.

"Did you know this nigga killed our sister?"

"Audrey?" she asked, as her brows furrowed even more. She remembered the Danger siblings being super tight-knit. There was no way Remington did what he was accused of. He was the oldest, and he took care of his siblings. He loved them. She remembered many nights in the farm house where all he would talk about were his siblings. She had never met them back then, but she felt as though she knew them because of how much Remington spoke of them. Fallon looked at Remington, and she saw a flash of regret in his eyes that made her tense, but before she could ask a clarifying question, Remington lunged for Kendrick. The blow to his nose knocked him back, and Remington was on him in a flash. "Don't speak her name, nigga! You know as well as I do I had no idea that would happen! I loved my baby sister!"

Kendrick was finally able to get from under his brother, and when he did, he stood quickly and delivered a kick to Remington's side that made him fly into the air before he landed back on his feet.

"I don't know shit, nigga! For all I know, you knew the risk and took it anyway!" Kendrick bellowed, and they charged each other again. Fallon glanced at the gang, and they looked like they were ready to jump in. She couldn't have that. She quickly placed herself between them and shoved Remington back. She didn't think she used a lot of force, but once again, the nigga was airborne. She didn't stop to see how he landed. She turned to Kendrick and held him back.

"Stop it!" she said harshly.

Kendrick struggled against her, then he looked down at her in shock before saying, "How the fuck are you so strong?"

He pushed against her again, but she didn't budge. He was used to being the strongest nigga in the room, but both her and Remington had him beat.

"Are you done?" she asked, but this time she spoke kinder. Her eyes were watery with tears because the emotion of this entire situation was a lot, but she blinked them away and waited for his answer. Finally, he nodded, and she nodded back before turning to Remington, who was now directly behind her breathing heavily as he mugged Kendrick. "Remy."

He looked down at her. It didn't matter that his brother was a threat. When Fallon called, he would take his eyes off an army of enemies to attend to her. "What happened?"

He looked into her eyes and knew what she was asking. He knew the weight of her question. He clenched his jaw before placing a hand on her cheek. Automatically, without thinking about anyone else in the room, she leaned into him. When they heard Kendrick scoff behind them, they practiced restraint and separated. Remington kept his eyes on Fallon but his words were for his brother. "Fallon created vampirism."

Kendrick stumbled back a little as if he had been hit before saying, "Impossible."

Scarlette stepped forward and looked at her best friend skeptically. "He's right... that's impossible."

Fallon shook her head sadly. "He's right. I was... I am... no. I was a witch."

Remington placed a hand at the small of her back discreetly and rubbed in slow circles. "You still are, my love."

She shook her head. "I don't have any magic. I—"

"Once a witch, always a witch," he assured.

"What the fuck are you two even talking about?" Kendrick seethed before looking at Fallon. "How could you not tell me about this?"

Everyone looked at her, waiting for an answer. Fallon fidgeted from foot to foot because not only was she in the hot spot, the thirst she felt was clawing at her insides. She felt like she was going insane. Remington studied her and said, "She's thirsty."

"Fuck that!" Kendrick snapped. "I need some

fuckin' answers! Did you know who I was this entire time?"

Remington stepped forward, but Fallon put an arm out to stop him. She looked up at him and whispered, "It's okay." He looked down at her in concern before nodding his head curtly. Fallon looked at Kendrick and said, "I didn't remember anything until I woke up a few minutes ago. I had no idea who you or Remington were. I swear to you."

He shook his head, and Fallon could see the distrust in his eyes, which saddened her, but she couldn't blame him.

"Fallon and I were lovers. I kept her a secret from everyone because she was a witch. You remember how it was back then, brother," Remington said.

"I'm not your brother," Kendrick snapped.

Remington's jaw flexed, but he continued after a moment. "All we wanted was a lifetime of freely being together. Fallon is a part of the Bordeaux coven. You know they are the most powerful coven in existence. She was able to create a potion that would allow us to be immortal… living freely to love one another. We would be stronger than any human and outrun them if need be. The night we took it, I survived, but Fallon didn't. What I realized later, my love, was I should have bitten you. You were never meant to survive the potion. Fate couldn't have it that way. Two people could not be created by the potion but one person could and our mating bond would have done the rest. We didn't know about the mating logistics before, though. Unfortunately, I found out the hard way..."

"Yeah, you killed our fuckin' sister!" Kendrick roared. Fallon could tell the story he just heard was entirely too much for him to bare, so he clung on to the only part of the story he'd already known... the story of Remington turning his family.

Remington nodded before saying, "And I've regretted that shit every day for the last damn near thousand years."

His mind went to a dark place... a place he didn't often think about. He walked over to the chair in the corner where he spent the past few days waiting for Fallon to wake up as he told the most painful memory he had.

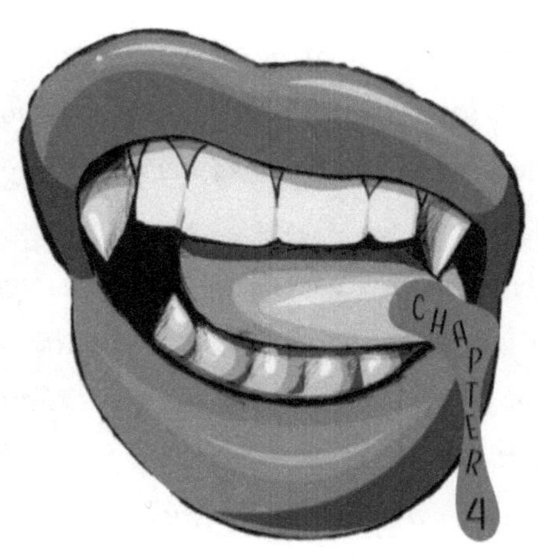

Over nine hundred years ago

"FALLON... FALLON? MY LOVE, WAKETH UP!" *Remington kneeled over Fallon as he shook her violently, attempting to wake her up. Deep down, he knew it was of no use. Her body was cold, and the smell of decaying flesh wafted through the air. He looked around wildly, wondering how long he had been out. The last thing he remembered was taking the potion with Fallon, and then there was nothing but pain and thirst. Had it been days? Years? Hours? He had no clue. Judging by Fallon's body, though, it had been at least a couple of days.*

A sob tore through Remington's chest as he pounded the ground beside Fallon's body. It shocked him when the dirt ground beneath him cracked from the blows. He pulled his hand away and stared at it in wonder as tears still streamed from his eyes. Still on his knees, he looked down at the love of his life and brushed her wild ginger hair out of her face.

"What hath happened?" he whispered as agony settled in his heart. He knew he would never be the same again. The void that filled him now was too great. Fallon was his everything, and she was no more. Pain rocked his heart as he bent down to kiss her for a final time. As he leaned closer to her, he caught a whiff of something mixed in with the smell of his beloved's rotting flesh. He sniffed her, right by the neck, and his tongue automatically licked out at the pointed teeth he'd just noticed resting in his mouth. "What is happening?"

The urge to... bite Fallon was strong, and it confused him. Then, it dawned on him. "I must drinketh human blood."

He remembered the stipulations of taking the potion, and his stomach both churned and growled at the idea. He pulled back, but then immediately lunged forward, his thirst getting the best of him. When his fangs tore through Fallon's flesh, he moaned. In the back of his mind, the part that was still used to being human, he fought against what he was doing. He knew it wasn't natural, and he knew it was morbid, but he also couldn't ignore the strength he felt filling his body with every gulp. He stayed crouched over Fallon for several minutes until there was no more blood left in her body. Tears streamed down his face as he stumbled back. "What has't I done?"

He scooted away from Fallon until his back hit a pig pen. He could vividly hear their heartbeats, and he used his hands to cup his ears, not used to all the sounds surrounding him. After several long moments, he heard feet nearing the farm house. They sounded light, but what overrode that sound was the steady heartbeat and blood flowing through the person's body. If he had to guess, it was a woman. As soon as she entered the farm house, from the looks of it to start her chores for the day, Remington was on her. He moved quicker than she could blink, and he stumbled on his feet a little, shocked at how quickly he moved, but he didn't let that stop him. He looked at the woman, who had fallen back on her ass and was shaking with fear.

"My deepest apologies," he murmured before lunging on top of the woman and biting her neck. Her scream was cut off, and she completely relaxed. It surprised Remington when she moaned, and it caused him to as well. Her blood was warm, unlike Fallon's had been, and she tasted heavenly. More strength seemed to enter his body the more he drank. After a moment, the woman screamed, and it startled him, but still, he kept drinking until there was nothing left. He dropped her body and moved away, covering his face with his hands. "What has't thee done to me, Fallon?"

He couldn't control the thirst, and it terrified him. He

didn't want to be a monster. Maybe if Fallon were alive, he would be able to handle this. She made him stronger in many ways, but she was dead, which caused him to spiral out of control. He felt as though he were going crazy, and he wondered if it was better to take his own life. He wondered if he even could, but that thought was cut short when someone moaned. His hands fell from his face as he peered up, and his eyes landed on the woman he'd just killed... only, she wasn't dead at all. She was sitting up and squinting around before her eyes landed on him and grew wider. She scooted away from him, and they both noticed how fast she moved. It was so quick and harsh that she crashed against a stall with horses and broke the wood, allowing the horses to break free from their jails. Neither of them cared about the horses running about. Remington stared at her before his eyes trailed to Fallon. He wondered with a great amount of hope if she would wake back up, too. While he peered at his lover, the other woman tried making a mad dash, but Remington was faster. It wasn't lost on him how strong the woman was, and as she bared her teeth at him, he realized she had become what he was. That scared him. He didn't know the woman nor what her intentions would be with such power. In a panic and before he could stop himself, he grasped her head and gave a light tug. That light tug pulled her head clean off, and he dropped it at the same time her body fell to the ground.

"No..." he whispered as he fell to his knees. "No..."

He rocked back and forth, fully convinced that he had lost his mind completely. Several moments later, he pushed his pain and confusion aside to come up with a plan. He knew he couldn't stay there too long because someone would come looking for the woman. He also did not want them to find her body mutilated like it was. He feared they would blame the witches, and if he could do nothing else, he would protect Lily... Fallon's sister. His heart pained at the thought of her. He knew she had to be worried about her sister.

Finally, after several long moments, he gently picked Fallon's body from the ground and quickly moved her outside the farm house door. After making sure the coast was clear, he went back inside and let all the animals out of the farmhouse. They ran free in the fields next to the building, and that satisfied him. He may be a monster now, but he still had some heart left. Lastly, he gathered the stone and flint he and Fallon used sometimes to make a fire in the cold months. It took him one try to strike fire near a pile of hay, and he wasted no time grabbing the ignited elements and tossing them on the head and body of the woman he killed. He struck another fire and then another, scattering the burning hay around the farmhouse.

Once he was satisfied that the farm house and the body would burn to ash, he picked Fallon up again and made his way home, a new plan forming in his mind.

A grassy area in the woods outside the Danger dwelling served as a resting place for Fallon.

"I'll beest backeth for thee," Remington whispered, crouching next to her and caressing her cheek. In his mind, Fallon would wake up any minute and join him on this new adventure, and while he allowed her to rest, he was going to ensure the other people he loved could remain with him always.

After one last look at Fallon, he stood and made his way toward the dwelling. The sun was rising, so he knew it was early morning. His parents would surely be awake, and so would Kendrick. Audrey, on the other hand, who was only thirteen, would most likely be asleep until their mother woke her for her chores, but Remington would likely wake her first.

When he walked inside, it surprised him to see his parents sitting in the wooden chairs Remington made for his family so they could eat dinner together at the table. Kendrick and Audrey were both still asleep in the corner where the siblings rested, Audrey's head lying on Kendrick's arm. It looked as though she had been crying, and Remington wondered why, but it hit him... they were worried about him. His parents, however, looked angry.

They rose when they saw him, and immediately, his father questioned him.

"Where has't thee been?" Maximus grabbed Remington by his collar and hemmed him up. Remington let him, reverting back to his former self... his weak self. His father ruled his house with an iron fist. The three Danger children were not to step a toe out of line or complain of their duties, or they would be beaten. When Remington saw his father raise his fist, out of reflex he grabbed his wrist, and Maximus struggled against him, looking at him in surprise. Remington's eyes grew wide as if he had forgotten his reason for coming home in the first place. His strength against his father reminded him, and without thinking about it, he leaned in and bit his father's neck. He was convinced that simply biting a human would turn him like him. Afterall, that was what happened to the woman in the farm house.

Prima couldn't see what was happening. She only assumed her husband was whispering harsh words in Remington's ear, as to not wake the other children. When she heard her husband cry out, she took a step forward, concerned. "My love?"

When he didn't respond, she took another step, but halted when her husband's body fell to the ground, and Remington stood there wiping his mouth of... blood. The scream that built its way up her throat died when, in a flash, Remington was right in front of her, grasping her arms. "T'll only did hurt for a moment."

Of course, Remington didn't know that, but judging by how little the woman at the farm house and his father struggled against him, he assumed this process didn't hurt too much. He was barely able to register the fear on his mother's face before he bit her.

"Remington?"

He heard his brother's voice, but he ignored him, intent on finishing his mother so he could get to him and Audrey. After a few moments, his mother cried out and struggled against him before going completely limp. He took great care to lay her down gently before turning on his brother, who was waking Audrey and telling her they had to run. Kendrick didn't know what was going on with his brother, or why he had been missing for so long, but he'd changed. The energy exuding from him was powerful and wicked, and Kendrick would do whatever he could to save his sister.

"Brother, steadfast," Remington said as he wiped his mouth and advanced slowly on his siblings.

Kendrick stumbled back just as Audrey woke, rubbing her eyes, but when they landed on Remington, a smile broke out on her pretty face. Oh, how she looked like their mother with smooth skin and long curly hair. She jumped up quicker than Kendrick could react and raced over to Remington, who snatched her in a tight hug.

"Where has't thee been?" she asked, her brown eyes peering up at Remington.

He smoothed her wild hair away from her face and smiled down at her before looking at Kendrick, who stood so frozen in fear he couldn't even call out to his sister.

"Trusteth me," Remington said while making eye contact with his brother. He bared his fangs, and in a flash, he bit Audry, who didn't put up a fight, not even after minutes passed. That was how much trust she had in her big brother. She knew he wasn't intentionally hurting her, so she succumbed to the pain, allowing it to flow through her.

Kendrick shouted for his brother to stop. He begged him, but Remington didn't until every last drop of blood was taken from her body. He laid her down gently alongside their mother and advanced on Kendrick, who was now in fight or flight mode. His eyes scanned the dim one room dwelling, looking for an escape, but to do so, he would have to go through the monster in front of him. He was resigned to fight, so he put his fists up, and Remington shook his head. "Fret not, brother."

"Thee murderer!" Kendrick bellowed, tears streaming down his face as he looked at his family scattered across the floor. "Behold what thee've done!"

Remington glanced behind him then faced his brother with a knowing smile. "Trusteth me," he repeated before lunging for Kendrick and biting him on the neck.

Moments later, Kendrick joined his family on the floor, and Remington smiled at his handy-work. It didn't take long for his father to stir, and excitement filled Remington as he watched his father look around in confusion. Before Remington could say anything, Prima rose as well, almost as if she could feel her husband's confusion and wanted to aid him.

"My love," she gasped as Maximus gathered her in his arms.

Remington allowed them their moment before taking a step toward them. "Mama, Papa—"

"Stop!" Maximus bellowed, and immediately, Remington did. No matter how hard he tried moving his feet, they stayed planted in place, but it only lasted a few moments before he was able to break free. He looked at his father with a furrowed brow and said, "Audrey and Kendrick shall beest waking soon."

Prima glanced at her other children, and a cry tore from her chest as she ran to them. The anger within Maximus's eyes was palpable, and in a flash, he stood and hemmed Remington against the wall, only this time, the stone from the dwelling crumbled under his force, and the two landed on top of it while Maximus scrambled back. "What hath thee done?"

Remington stood, unfazed by the blow, and walked over the crumbled stone toward his father. Before he could reply, Prima cried out with joy as Kendrick rose. She *wrapped him in her embrace and rocked him back and forth for a few moments while Maximus and Remington watched on. Remington felt victorious, but Kendrick shattered that when he glanced at Audrey's body. He pushed his mother off him, and she slid several feet on her butt, only to rotate to her feet and run with her newfound speed back toward her daughter's body. "Audrey, my love... waketh thee!"*

Remington's smile faltered as he watched his brother and mother shake his sister's body. She should have woken prior to Kendrick, but maybe she just needed a little longer.

Long minutes passed as the family grieved over Audrey's body while Remington watched in horror, losing hope as the minutes ticked by. After an hour, his father stood with tears in his eyes and turned on Remington. "What hath thee done?"

Remington responded without meaning to. "I gaveth thee immortal life, strength, hearing, and speedeth. 'Tis calledeth vampirism. Thee has't to feedeth off humans to survive by using thy fangs to drinketh their blood—"

Immediately, he stopped talking as the power of his tongue returned to him. He looked at his father in confusion. Remington didn't even think his father knew the odd control he had over him.

"Who doth this to thee?" he demanded after several long moments of processing what his son said.

"Fallon Bordeaux, thee witch—" He clamped his hand over his mouth, not believing he just told on the love of his life. What was wrong with him? How was his father doing this? He wondered if he had the same power, but as he opened his mouth to speak, his mother rushed him and knocked him back, slapping his face and then grasping his arms roughly, bellowing about Audrey, who had yet to wake. Remington wanted to fight back, but searing pain overtook his entire body before everything faded to black.

"PRIMA FOUND out about her gift when she touched you," Kendrick mumbled. "She kept doing the shit over and over again, every time your bones would regenerate. She was mad as fuck at you. We all were. The process lasted months while we figured out how this vampirism shit worked, but then winter rolled around, and we started getting sick. It was natural instinct to flee west, and when we got to warmer climate, we knew what we needed to do to get rid of you once and for all."

"The cold doesn't affect me like it does y'all," Remington said, and Fallon was pretty sure she was the only one who saw him swipe the lone tear from his eye before speaking. Her heart broke for him as tears streamed down her own face. The agony he must have felt when the potion failed her and when he accidentally killed his sister. She knew how much

Remington loved his family back then, even his father who was an asshole. All he wanted to do was please them and love on them. He wanted that so badly, he turned them without fully understanding what he was doing because he wanted to be with them for an eternity, and that shit had backfired on him.

Kendrick nodded. "You don't think I don't know that, nigga? In case you didn't know, my gift is foresight. I knew you weren't affected by the cold like us, and I knew you would only stay there for a certain amount of time before your pity party was up. I also knew you wouldn't bother us after leaving the cold, and I was fine with that. Too bad I thought that meant for an eternity. I haven't been able to foresee you in centuries. Sometimes this bullshit ass gift pisses me off. "

He mumbled that last part, and Fallon felt her heart ache for him, too. She couldn't imagine the pain he must have felt witnessing his brother kill his sister and turn the rest of his unwilling family caused him. It really was no wonder he hated his brother and never mentioned him, but Fallon knew Remington's heart. At least, she knew it back then. As pitiful as it sounded, everything Remington did was an accident. He really didn't know any better, and had he, he wouldn't have taken the risk. If they really thought about it, this was all her fault. That realization caused a permanent ache to settle in her heart.

"I've kept up with you over the years, nigga. I know what your gift is. Only reason I showed my face again was because of her," Remington replied, inclining his head toward Fallon. "For what it's worth, I've suffered a great deal and spent all this time in complete solitude… never turning anyone, and keeping my distance. I regret what I did, Kendrick, whether you believe it or not."

Fallon gazed up at Remington, and she could tell that was the most vulnerable he'd been in a very very long time. Probably since the night they took the vampirism potion. She refrained from reaching up and caressing his cheek, but oh, how she longed to. She wanted to feel him with her new fingers. She wanted to take her time re-learning him. Above all that… she wanted blood. She cleared her throat again, and listened as Remington continued.

"I've wondered over the years why I didn't have control over my thirst those first few days. I'm pretty sure it was the power of the potion still working its way through my system. I couldn't help the amount of blood I drank. It was like each time, I couldn't stop until a body was drained. It wasn't until I left the Antartica that I realized I didn't need to kill in order to survive."

"I remember my thirst being stronger back then, too," Kendrick admitted before clearing his throat and glaring at his brother. "I didn't kill anyone, though."

"It would have been stronger for him," Fallon said defensively. She understood how magic worked. She remembered. It was always stronger when it was first born. Any potion or spell was more powerful within the first few days before it slipped into its comfortability. She suspected that was why the first few vampires created were turned quickly and had better odds at surviving. Kendrick confirmed as much when he spoke his next words, completely ignoring Fallon. "People were easier to turn back then, too, and it was as if the mating bond didn't truly exist. That didn't settle until years later when less and less people turned, and it started becoming common knowledge among the vamps that if someone turned, it was because of a bond... like fate."

He glanced at Fallon with pain in his eyes before standing and looking at Remington with hate in his eyes. "You came back for her? She's yours now. Y'all can fuckin' leave now."

"Kendrick," Fallon gasped, but she was met with Kendrick's back as he left the room. Axel followed close behind, and Scarlette and Papa looked torn.

Fallon's heart broke, as a piece of it walked out that door with Kendrick, but she didn't have time to dwell on it because Remington was turning her to face him and gathering her in his arms.

They looked into each other's eyes, and there was a millennia of anguish shifting between the two, but Remington refrained from diving into that. He hadn't had these types of feelings in a very long time, and he felt a bit misplaced. The man Fallon once knew was dead, but the love he carried for her was just as fresh and real as it had been over nine hundred years ago. "You're thirsty, my love."

Fallon sighed at hearing the old nickname he used to call her, and a giggle bubbled up from the surface. Remington looked down at her in confusion as Papa finally found his voice. "This bitch has gone loony."

Another giggle erupted from her, and she turned to Papa. "No, I was just reminded about the way we used to speak back then when he called me my love."

A grin formed on Remington's lips when she turned to him again. "A lot has changed since then, huh?" Fallon nodded before clearing her throat again and shifting uncomfortably. "You're thirsty, my love."

Fallon peered up at him with sadness in her eyes. In this lifetime, the last thing she wanted to do was become a vampire and feed off humans. It was odd to know that she was the one responsible for creating the creatures in the first place, and she was eager to take the potion back then. Now, she battled with herself on the thought of feeding off humans, but she was resigned to knowing that was the only way she could survive. As she looked up at Remington, she realized there was nothing more than she wanted than to survive… with him. For him. She nodded curtly, and Scarlette spoke up this time. "Looks like its time to show her how to feed."

At Scarlette's words, Papa rushed out of the room and then the house. He was gone for all of fifteen minutes, while Scarlette pried Fallon from Remington's arms and hugged her best friend. Remington retreated to his former seat in the corner of the room, allowing the women to have their moment, but still keeping his eye on Fallon. He had lost her once, and that cost him many lifetimes of suffering. There was no way he would lose her again, which meant she was to stay under his watchful gaze.

Papa finally returned with petite blond woman.

Fallon could hear the girl's heart pumping and the blood rushing through her veins, and it snatched her attention away from Scarlette, who was bouncing around on the bed, excited that Fallon woke up and would be alive for an eternity.

Fallon jumped off the bed at the same time Remington hopped up from his seat. He was at her side in half a second, and he placed a hand at her waist while she bared her fangs.

"Woah, she's really thirsty," Papa commented.

"Thirsty—"

"Shhh…" Papa said, cutting the blond girl off. "Don't worry about it, mami." He turned toward Remington and said, "Coach her through it quickly so we can get this girl out of here."

"Where'd you even find her? And how did you get her to agree to come with you?" Remington asked, amused.

"His unofficial gift is the gift of gab. We don't question it, we just rock with it," Scarlette said, dismissing Remington.

"Coach her through this so we can send this beauty on her way," Papa said, pulling blond strand of hair out of the stranger's face.

"Coach her through what? I thought we were—"

Remington cut the poor girl off again when he spoke to Fallon. "Bite her neck, my love. The venom will do the rest. Drink until you're full, and don't be nervous. The magic has settled surrounding us vampires. You don't have to kill unless you want to."

Fallon listened to what he was saying, but she focused on the girl's neck, now that it was visible since Papa pushed her hair out of the way. Remington was barely finished speaking when Fallon's thirst took over, and she lunged for the girl. Her scream was cut off when Fallon sank her teeth into her neck and the venom worked its way into her bloodstream. The girl moaned in pleasure, and Fallon smiled against her neck as she carefully took her first sip of blood. It tasted good as hell, and she immediately felt her thirst dissipate some. Her hearing sharpened, and strength filled her as she greedily drank more. She almost felt delirious with thirst, but when she felt full, she pulled back, staring at the girl, who simply smiled at Fallon dumbly.

"Good job, blondie," Papa said, patting the girl on the back and escorting her out of the room.

"How do you feel?" Remington asked, coming up beside her and thumbing blood away from the corner of her mouth.

"Amazing," Fallon replied, smiling up at him and then feeling guilty for smiling when Kendrick was somewhere with a broken heart. Just that quickly, the thirst she felt overshadowed every other feeling, and she wasn't sure how she felt about that.

"I remember my first feed," Papa replied whimsically as he sauntered over to the bed and fell onto it, back first. "It was magical. I feel like I've been chasing that high ever since."

"What happened to the girl?" Fallon asked skeptically.

Papa waved her off. "I found her at the store a few miles from here and coaxed her into driving me home then convinced her to have a drink with me as thanks. Little did she know, *she* was the drink. Anyway, she's on her way home, none the wiser."

Fallon looked at the other vamps surrounding her before asking, "Will I ever get used to this?"

"Oh, baby," Scarlette said, grasping Fallon by the shoulders. "You will. Promise. How about we spend the day doing cool vampire things? Huh? It'll give Kendrick and Axel the house to themselves to… do whatever they want. Bro time, you know?"

Remington snorted at that. "I'm his brother."

"Barely," Scarelette muttered.

"Touche," Remington replied.

Fallon shifted uncomfortably. "As good as that sounds… I need to handle something else first."

Remington knew what she was going to say before she even said it, and he braced himself because as much as he'd been keeping up with his family all these years, he'd been keeping up with the witches, too. He wasn't sure how well Fallon would be taken, but he also knew her well enough to know that this shit was something she would be adamant about.

"What's that?" Papa asked, curiously, while Scarlette waited for her to reply.

"I need to go see my grandmother."

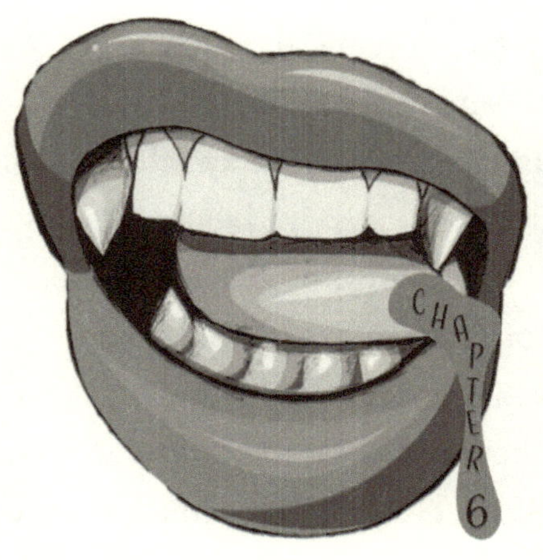

THE CAR RIDE to her grandmother's was the first time Fallon and Remington had been alone in over nine hundred years. Getting Scarlette and Papa to stay behind was a challenge, and if Fallon felt she could have gotten away with asking Remington to stay behind, she would have. She knew better, though. Not only did the mating bond allow them a special awareness surrounding each other, she knew him. It may have been a long time, and he may have changed a lot since the last time they'd seen each other, but at the core, he was still the same Remington. He would do anything to protect her… even back then. She knew there was no way she would be able to do anything on her own for a very long time. Simply thinking about the pain he had to endure caused anguish to overtake Fallon's body, so she understood why he wouldn't want to leave her side, even without him speaking... and he hadn't. Neither of them had, even though there was so much to hash out and talk about. It was as if the anxiety about Fallon facing her grandmother filled the space between them, keeping them from addressing the last nine hundred years apart.

When they pulled up to her grandmother's home, Fallon smiled. Despite her childhood being somewhat tragic with the loss of her parents, she had nothing but fond memories. The ones that were hard to think about were when she got older and started dating Kendrick. She cringed at the thought because she now had a better understanding of why her grandmother was so against Kendrick.

Remington placed a hand on her thigh after he parked the car and took her in. Despite feeling shy under his gaze, Fallon matched his stare. He could tell she was nervous, and he was a little confused on why. "What happened between you two?"

Fallon stiffened as the weight of the fallout between she and her grandmother sat on her shoulders. Perspective was everything, and sometimes, ignorance was not bliss. Had Fallon had all her memories, she knew things would have played out differently in her life, and she wondered if that was a good thing or a bad thing. Before she could dive deep into her mind and spiral from her thoughts, Remington said, "Fallon?"

Her name on his lips snapped her out of her thoughts and caused her to focus solely on him. "Kendrick used to tell me about the way The Guild treated witches. I never thought anything of it because I didn't realize it had anything to do with me, but in reality… it has everything to do with me. My grandmother disowned me when Kendrick and I started dating… now, I know why. I thought it was just because she didn't like him. I didn't realize she knew all about vampires… shit."

Fallon closed her eyes and let her head fall against the headrest. Her mind was swarming with thoughts and memories, all while trying to adjust to her new senses since becoming a vampire. Remington was out of the car and opening her car door within a second, causing Fallon's eyes to pop back open. He unbuckled her seatbelt and pulled her up into his arms. She clung to him and breathed him in. "I can't believe you're here."

"I looked for you, baby," Remington murmured against her hair. "I kept up with your coven, and I waited for you to be born again. I—"

"I know," Fallon whispered as she tilted her head up to look at him. She could feel the anguish in his energy. His pain was palpable. She didn't need him to plead his case to her. She understood without him saying another word. She pulled away slightly and grabbed his hand. "There will be time to talk about us later, I promise. Let's face my grandmother first."

He swallowed the lump in his throat before turning to face the house. It looked small, but Fallon knew better. As a child, she always tried to figure out how the yellow house looked so small on the outside but was big on the inside. Now, she understood. She could feel the magic radiating from the lot her childhood home stood on. Together, they took a step toward the front door, but in the blink of an eye, they were bound by their hands and feet and sitting in a cold cellar. Fallon's eyes widened as she looked around frantically.

"What the fuck?" she voiced in a panic as she tried to pull her hands apart from behind her back, but a stinging sensation rocking up her arm and straight to her brain stopped her.

"Don't fight it, baby," Remington gritted. "It's a spell. It mimics freezing temperatures. It's a witches oldest trick in the book. It hurts more when you move around."

Fallon tried to recall such a spell in her last lifetime or prior, but she came up with nothing before she realized it was most likely created after the birth of vampires. "How—"

Fallon stopped talking when she heard footsteps coming down the stairs to the left of her. A warm raspy voice filled her ears, and Fallon's sad smile was immediate.

"You thought you could run up on me in my own house?"

The old lady with long silver hair braided over one shoulder stopped short when she made eye contact with Fallon. Her hazel eyes widened before they flicked over to Remington and turned into slits. "You're a Danger. I've never seen you before."

"Grandma," Fallon breathed, cutting off whatever Remington was going to say.

Her grandmother's eyes rolled back to her granddaughter, and Fallon could see unshed tears as she spoke. "What did they do to you, baby?"

Fallon shook her head as tears of her own crowded her eyes. "I'm so sorry, grandmother... Lily... I'm so sorry."

Remington's head snapped toward her as his own eyes widened before he looked at the old lady standing several feet away just at the bottom of the stairs.

"Lily?" he asked incredulously. He knew witches were reborn into the same coven mixed with new witches all the time. It was how a coven grew. What he didn't know was that the woman before him had been Fallon's younger sister in her last lifetime. Guilt immediately plagued Remington. The young girl he was supposed to protect in honor of Fallon all those years ago was standing in front of him. Remington wasn't a person who felt shame... but at that moment, the unfamiliar emotion had him in a chokehold.

Once again, Lily's piercing hazel eyes found Remington. "You say my name like you know me. You know me, boy?" Her accent was thick. She was NOLA through and through. He could tell she had been settled here for many lifetimes. Before he could reply, she took a step closer to the two vampires and pointed at Fallon. "Did you do this to her?"

"I—"

"Grandma, please... let us free so we can explain," Fallon urged.

Lily looked at Fallon for several long moments, her eyes squinting and appraising her granddaughter before she finally spoke. "You remember, don't you?"

Fallon always used to wonder how her grandmother seemed to know her every thought and everything that was going on with her. Now, she understood because that same magic was within her. Witches were very intuitive and very rarely wrong when it came to emotions. True empaths were what they were. Fallon nodded, and before she could blink, her grandmother waved her hand lazily, and the three of them were sitting in the living room. Fallon's hands and feet were free, but one glance to the left of her where Remington sat on the couch, and she noted he was still tied up. She sighed and looked at Lily. "Grandma—"

"His bondage stays," Lily snapped in a clipped tone with finality before walking slowly toward Fallon and gathering her face into her hands. She peered down at her granddaughter before pulling her top lip up slightly, revealing a pointed fang. She shook her head sadly. "I knew it was only a matter of time when you started dating Kendrick Danger. You've always been so hardheaded."

Fallon smiled. A few days ago she would have been hurt by her grandmother's harsh words, but now, she understood them in their entirety. Fallon remembered many lifetimes where she and Lily existed together. They were what the coven described as twin flames. When one was born, the other would surely pop up in the same lifetime. There had been one lifetime where they were even twins. Both were stubborn in their own right, but they always respected one another. The never changed. Fallon tentatively stood and embraced her grandmother, tears finally falling. "I've missed you."

And they each understood that she meant more than just the past few years when they hadn't spoken. Fallon had missed her for many lifetimes. She could feel Lily's magic. It had grown stronger in the last nine hundred years, which meant she had lived many lifetimes… without her.

Lily pulled back and asked, "How much do you remember?"

"Every single lifetime," Fallon said with a sad smile. "Even the last one."

Lily nodded and sat in the chair away from Remington. Fallon knew she didn't trust him, and she didn't blame her. Lily regarded the couple before asking, "What happened? Why have you not been back?"

The pain in Lily's voice caused Fallon's heart to crack wide open. The thought of Lily living several lifetimes without her twin flame was torturous. She realized Lily must have been so happy when Fallon was born, only to quickly realize Fallon hadn't remembered her. Lily had lived a saddened life this go around, and Fallon felt responsible.

Hunching her shoulders, Fallon leaned forward and said, "I'm not sure, Grandma."

Although the two lived many lives together and

knew each other as many different roles in each life, a coven rule was to always address a family member as they were in that lifetime. Their roles were absolute in each lifetime and to be respected.

"What do you know, Fallon?" Lily asked with her hands clasped in front of her.

Fallon glanced at Remington before responding to her grandmother. "Grandma... I don't know how else to say this but to just say it... Back then, Remington and I were in a relationship. It's hard for me to explain the connection we have—"

"You don't have to explain. I can feel it," Lily spat with disdain, and Fallon nodded. She understood Lily's perspective. She also understood that what she was about to say next would rock her world.

Fresh tears gathered in Fallon's eyes as she said, "Lily... I'm the one that created vampirism. All those years ago... I created it by potion so I could live with Remington for an eternity without being crucified."

Lily blinked slowly. "Excuse me?"

Her accent grew thicker depending on how passionate the conversation was. Right now, it was about as thick as it could get.

Fallon hung her head. "We each took the potion, and it worked for Remington, but it didn't for me. I died in transition."

Lily's eyes flashed angrily toward Remington. "So you decided to kill me?"

Fallon's head whipped toward Remington, waiting on his response. She never knew what became of Lily back then. She didn't even think to ask. As she looked at Remington and the way his jaw clenched as he looked directly at Lily, her hart dropped.

"Remy?" she whispered.

His eyes found hers before shaking his head slightly and focusing back on Lily. "I vowed to protect you. I had every intention on doing so. Back then... when it all started, I didn't know how any of it worked. I turned my family, and my sister died in the process. My parents were so enraged, and that was when we learned of our gifts. Only the original vampires have them. My father's is compulsion. He didn't even know what he was doing at the time, but when he asked me a question, I had no choice but to answer. He asked who did this to me, and I said a witch."

"And they found our coven and killed us all," Lily replied dryly. "So, you're Maximus and Prima's son? Which would make you Kendrick's brother?" Her brow was raised as she asked the question, and Fallon was lost in thought at the horror of what happened. Remington nodded, and Lily asked, "And

I have never heard of you because they disowned you after you turned them and killed their daughter?"

"Correct," Remington replied. "I loved Fallon then, and I still do now. Like you, I waited lifetime after lifetime for her to be reborn. When I found out my brother was getting married, I came to check in. I didn't plan on intervening until I saw her... I had nine hundred years to ponder over why the potion did not work for her. I promised myself I would correct things and set us on the path we started all those years ago. I knew in my heart she was my mate, so I bit her. It took her a few days to turn, and I worried I had killed her... but she's here now, and she remembers everything."

Lily stared at the couple and grunted in response. Fallon looked between the two. "I had no idea Maximus and Prima killed you, Grandma. It's my fault—"

"It is," Lily agreed, and Fallon hung her head. "But I also remember the boy you used to rave about back then. I remember how in love you were. The night you went missing, you promised I would get to meet him soon and we would be a family. Mama and Papa had died, so you were all I had aside from our coven. I waited for you... but you never came. Instead, those monsters did. When I was reborn, the coven disbanded. We still keep in touch, but we are harder to find if we are separated. I've been born in New Orleans for three lifetimes now. You should see how the coven has grown."

It was the first time Lily's eyes lit up since the two vampires had been in the house. Fallon smiled warmly before letting go of Remington's hand and kneeling before her grandmother, resting her head in her lap. "I know I am now one of them, but I am also one of you. Can you accept me?"

Lily's lips set into a thin line before she placed a hand on Fallon's wild ginger hair and stroked it. "I can try. The vampires have caused a great deal of hurt over the years to our coven. They are still hunting us today… but my love for you has never wavered. You're hard headed and like going your own way. Always have been like that. It broke my heart when you chose Kendrick over me, but I had to remind myself that you were ignorant. You didn't know any better, but now you do. I'm expecting you to remember where your loyalty lies."

Fallon nodded. "I'm always loyal to you, Lily." She glanced back at Remington. "But he also has my loyalty."

Lily mugged Remington and spat, "I'll never like a Danger, but I'll try to tolerate him since he is exiled from his family. He just better not hurt you or this coven."

Remington chuckled, feeling a bit of relief at her words. "You have my word."

"Any chance you'll free him from his bonds now?" Fallon asked. It occurred to her that she could have done it, but she suddenly felt shy about her powers. She hadn't practiced in over nine hundred years. She used to be the most powerful witch in the coven, but she sadly knew that was no longer the case, and she didn't want to look like a fool in front of her grandmother or her mate.

Lily peered down at Fallon before shaking her head. "Not a chance."

With the wave of her hand, Remington disappeared, and Fallon stood quickly. "What did you do to him?"

"Hush, chile," Lily spoke before slowly rising from the chair she had been sitting in. "I only sent him back out to his car. I wanted to speak to you alone."

Fallon grabbed her grandmother's hands and asked, "What is it?"

"You've given me a lot to ponder today, Fallon, but one thing I do know is there's a war brewing, and you are at the center of it. I felt it the moment I laid eyes on you in the cellar. I don't know what the future holds, but I need you to tap into your higher self and trust your gut, you hear me? Don't trust anything but your gut. Those vampires are killers—"

"I'm one of them now," Fallon replied defiantly.

"Which makes you the acception. Witches are not killers unless it is for self defense, which means you cannot be a killer. Remember who you are. I don't care if your teeth are pointed now. You are a Bordeaux. A coven leader. Stick to your roots, chile, and try to stay discreet. The Guild hunts witches. If they find out you're a hybrid… they'll either want you dead or force you to be on their team so you can do their bidding."

"I hear you, Grandma… but not all vampires are bad—"

Lily held her hand up. "I believe that. I am not stupid, Fallon. Just as there are evil witches, I know there can be good vampires, but The Guild are not good vampires, and the company you are keeping are a little too close to The Guild for my liking. I won't sit here and debate with you. I just need you to stay safe and please… don't be a stranger. I have spent enough time without you, my dear."

Lily patted Fallon's cheek lovingly, and Fallon melted into the warmth of her hand. "I know, Grandma. I promise I won't be a stranger. Besides, I need your help tapping into my magic. It's been so long and—"

"Say no more. I can't imagine going what… eight hundred years without magic?"

"Over nine hundred," Fallon replied sadly.

"We will get you back on track," Lily replied, lifting Fallon's head with a finger to her chin. "Now, go. I have to call the coven and fill them in. Next time you come, don't bring that nigga."

Fallon barked out a laugh. "Grandma, I really would like you two to get to know each other."

"Aht! What did I say?" Lily snapped.

Fallon sighed and turned toward the door. "And you say I'm the hard headed one."

Lily swatted at Fallon's ass, and Fallon giggled before opening the front door. "I'll be back, Lily. Can you fix the defense on this place so I can come to the front door like a normal person?"

"I'll think about it, and don't take too long coming back, either. I want you to get back comfortable with your powers sooner rather than later."

Fallon nodded and blew her grandmother a kiss before making her way to the car where Remington sat, waiting patiently.

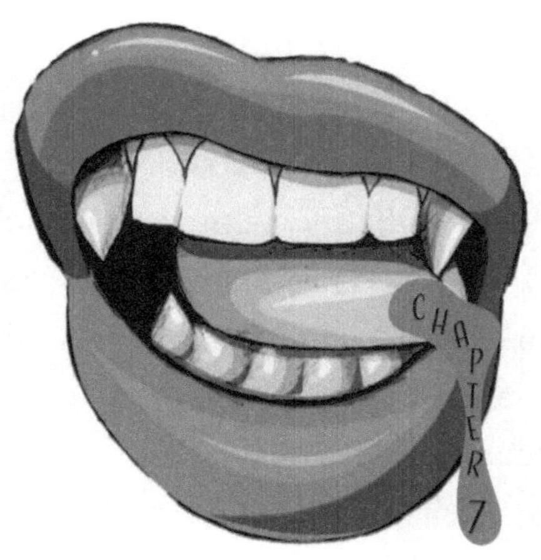

THE RIDE back to The Lair was silent. Fallon was lost in her thoughts about her coven, Lily, and the history between vampires and witches. It was so odd to her that she was the witch that started it all, yet she missed out on everything. Trying to wrap her mind around it was not an easy feat.

Remington pulled up to The Lair and cut the engine off, turning his body toward Fallon. He reached out and tucked a stray curl behind her ear before asking, "You okay?"

She sighed. "I should be asking you that. My grandmother did have you bound and magically transported around like it wasn't shit. I know that must have bothered a powerful vamp like yourself."

Remington chuckled. "I honestly expected more. I had no idea your grandmother was Lily. A little warning next time, okay, my love?"

Fallon melted into the seat as she gazed at Remington. She had yet to process that he was here... in front of her. She couldn't believe she had gone this entire lifetime without knowing who he was. "I didn't know I needed to warn you. You have to remember... I was dead when the fallout happened and the war between vampires and witches began."

He caressed her cheek. "I know. It doesn't matter, anyway. I'll take whatever animosity Lily has for me to the chin because I know I deserve that shit."

"No—"

"I do," Remington replied sternly. "I failed at protecting you both once. It won't happen again. I wouldn't even be mad at you if you hated me."

"Why would I hate you, Remy?" Fallon asked, genuinely confused.

He shrugged. "I lived and you didn't."

She grabbed his face and forced him to look at her. "And whose fault is that really?"

"It's not your fault," he replied as he clenched his jaw and tried to move his face out of her grasp. The cool thing about being a vampire now was that she wasn't a weak human. She held his face firmly, and he sighed heavily, blowing his minty breath all in her face.

She smiled lovingly at him. "It's my fault, Remy.

Stop blaming yourself. All this is my fault... let me own that."

He looked at a space just above her head and refused to agree, so Fallon pressed her forehead against his, prompting him to close his eyes completely. She caressed his cheek before speaking again. "You can't continue to blame yourself, my love. You have to unhand that burden. Let me carry it... the reason Audrey—"

"Don't," Remington snapped, but Fallon continued anyway.

"The reason Audrey is dead is because of me. Because of the potion I gave to you, and I'm sorry, baby. I am so so sorry. I wish I could take it back. I know how much you love your family—"

"Loved," Remington replied coldly.

Fallon shook her head. "I know how much you still love Audrey, even in death, and I know you love Kendrick, too. That shit doesn't go away simply because nine hundred years have passed. It doesn't work like that."

"He hates me. They all do, and I can't even blame them," Remington replied.

"You can, though. They know more than anyone how finicky this vampire shit was in the beginning. Hell, I didn't even know what I was getting us into, and I created it. Blame them for holding that against you. Blame me for making you trust in a potion that killed me and forced you into nine hundred years of solitude. Just stop blaming yourself."

Another lump formed in Remington's throat, and he coughed to clear it away before responding in the only way that felt natural to him. He kissed Fallon for the first time in over nine hundred years, and everything else fell away from them. The Lair disappeared from the background, the sounds of the critters in the grass and woods surrounding The Lair, the lingering smell of the gas from when the car was running… all of it fell away, and the only thing the two could sense was each other. The kiss was slow as their lips parted and their tongues got reacquainted. Everything about the moment was familiar yet fresh and exciting. When they finally pulled apart, they each wore sad smiles as they gazed into each others eyes, the world flooding back in as they thought about their time apart. Fallon thought about all the pain she caused so many people, especially him and now Kendrick, and Remington thought of his family and how he destroyed them.

Finally, Remington pulled away, and in a flash he was out of the car and at her side, opening her door and pulling her to his chest. Fallon looked up at the looming lair before asking, "Are you sure we should stay here? We kind of shook shit up… I'm not sure we are welcome anymore."

That thought hurt Fallon. The Lair had been her home for the past four years. It wasn't even so much the house she was attached to. It was the people. She hadn't spent a night away from the gang in years, and the thought of doing so now caused an ache to settle in her chest, but Remington squeezing her hand reassuringly made that ache hurt less. Everything was changing so quickly, and she wasn't sure how to feel, but sorting through her feelings didn't sound like such a bad idea. As if he could read her mind, he said, "I don't mind putting these mothafuckas in their place if you want to stay here. This is your home, too. I understand that, and my place is beside you, so they'll just have to fall in line either way, but if you'd rather be alone, I can make that happen, too. Alone, as in with me, of course."

Fallon cocked her head as she looked up at the love of her life with a slight smile. The question slipped from her lips before she could stop herself. She had been wondering how he was so much stronger than any other vampire and why his parents seemed to bow down to him. "All the originals have a gift… what's yours, Remy?"

He chuckled bitterly before muttering, "It's more like a curse."

"But what is it?"

"If I told you, you wouldn't believe me," he replied, and before she could push the subject, he said, "What's the plan? We staying here or not?"

She shook her head. "I think we should give Kendrick some space, and we have a lot to talk about. I'll just go in and grab some things and we can go… but Remy, I need to talk to Kendrick first. I can't just leave without speaking to him."

Remington nodded curtly, although he had yet to fully dissect the fact that his brother and mate had been fucking for the past four years. The thought made him mad as hell, so he shoved it away for a later time because he was honestly exhausted… mentally and emotionally. It had been a long ass few days, and the last thing he wanted to do was get into it with the gang again. "Whatever you need, my love."

Fallon squeezed his hand before guiding them into the house. Once they entered, Papa, Scarlette, and Axel were in the foyer in a flash.

"How was it?" Papa asked, nearly bouncing on his toes. "Got any cool witchy shit to show us?"

Scarlette shoved him to the side. "Papa, leave her alone. Can't you tell she's tired?"

Fallon chuckled softly as Scarlette pulled her best friend into her arms and hugged her tightly. Over

Scarlette's shoulder, Fallon met Axel's eyes, and she asked, "How is he?"

Scarlette let Fallon go, and everyone turned to look at Axel, waiting for his response. He shrugged with a stony face and said, "What can I say, Fal? You broke his heart."

Fallon could feel Remington behind her. Without even looking at him, she knew he was about to come to her defense on some rah rah shit. He had always been her protector, even all those years ago, but this version of him was harder. He really gave no fucks, and she knew she would have to be the one to tame his crazy ass. She put her hand up to stop him without even looking over her shoulder. When she felt Remington back down, she spoke. "Where is he? I won't disrespect him and stay here, but I don't want to leave without speaking to him."

Axel's jaw clenched as he peered at Fallon before he finally said, "He's in y'all's... your old room."

His words stung, but they were also true. That room was no longer hers and would never be again. It was Kendrick's before it was theirs, anyway. She nodded and turned to Remington. "Can you and Scarlette pack up my school stuff in the lab? She knows what to grab. I'll meet you down here in a few."

He shook his head. "Nah. I'm coming with you."

Fallon placed a hand on his chest. "No, baby. Please… I need to do this alone. I'm just going to pack up some things and talk to Kendrick. I'll be back shortly. I promise."

Remington looked like he wanted to object, but Fallon didn't give him a chance to. She glanced at Scarlette and nodded her head at her best friend. It was a wordless conversation between the two. *Don't let Remington follow me*, was what Fallon conveyed, and Scarlette understood. With that, Fallon turned on her heels and ran upstairs. It was definitely going to take some getting used to how fast she moved and how strong she was. She was knocking on Kendrick's door within two seconds and opening it another second later. After closing the door behind her, she faced Kendrick, who was lying on the couch that sat up against the wall. The TV was on, but he wasn't watching it. His arm was thrown over his eyes, and without looking at her he said, "Get out, Fallon."

She cringed at his tone, but she stayed where she was. "I just came to grab a few things."

He sat up and scoffed. "You leaving with that nigga?"

Fallon looked at him with tears in her eyes. "What do you want me to do, Kendrick?"

He shook his head before lying back down and ignoring her. Fallon nodded slowly before going into the closet and grabbing an oversized Louis Vuitton duffle bag. She stuffed clothes inside before going into the bathroom and grabbing her toiletries. When she finished with that, she slowly made her way back into the bedroom and grabbed her phone charger and purse before opening her nightstand drawer and grabbing some old photographs. After taking a look around, she was satisfied with the bag she packed, so she left the room and ran straight downstairs and out the door, throwing her bag in Remington's car before running back upstairs again, ignoring everyone on the way. When she made it back into the room, Kendrick was still in the same position. Determination settled in Fallon's core as she walked over to him and kneeled beside him. He groaned and sat up, causing Fallon to back up, but she remained kneeled in front of him. He glared down at her and asked, "The fuck do you want, Fallon?"

She shook her head before grabbing his hands. "I know you're hurting—"

"No, you don't fucking know." He squeezed her hands tightly and clenched his jaw so hard Fallon was sure at least one of his teeth would break in half. "You're the love of my life, man."

The way he whispered it was like a shock to Fallon's system. He sounded so broken, and to know she was the one that caused that type of pain in him rocked her. She wished there was something she could do to ease his pain. "Kendrick, I love you. I do. That doesn't just go away… but I can't be with you. You have to understand that—"

"I don't have to understand shit," he spat before pulling his hands from her grasp. He hoped he could talk some sense into her, but deep down even he knew it was no use. Mating bonds were the strongest kind of magic. Fate was what it was, and he knew his words couldn't change that, and that shit hurt him to his core. He just lost his everything, and he didn't know what was next for him.

Fallon opened her mouth to say something, but voices downstairs caused her to stop. They were muffled, but her new vamp hearing allowed her to hear just enough to know an argument was taking place. Kendrick and Fallon both sat and listened for a moment, trying to hear what was being said, but a loud crash caused them both to jump into action. Within seconds they were back in the foyer, and they came face to face with Prima and Maximus, along with several other members of The Guild.

"Ah, son. There you are… and I see your… *beloved* has finally woken," Prima stated.

Fallon's eyes swept across the room where Axel was standing against the wall. By his feet was broken glass and a broken end table. She realized that must have been the crash she heard. He was currently poised to fight, as were Scarlette and Papa. Remington was standing coolly off to the side, keeping his eyes shifting between his parents and Fallon.

She finally focused back on the king and queen, eying them wearily because she had no idea why they were here.

"What are you doing back here? I thought Remington sent you back to Jamaica," Kendrick snapped.

Maximus barked out a laugh. "Since when does The Guild bow down to one man?"

"Since this one man can kill you," Remington replied coolly.

Maximus cleared his throat before dismissing Remington. "Stand down, son. We aren't here for you. We're here for him."

Maximus pointed a long finger at Kendrick, and Fallon's nerves went haywire. Something wasn't right, and her intuition was on high alert. Out of the corner of her eye, she saw Axel take a step forward, but Prima stopped him with her words. "Another step, and I'll turn your bones to dust."

Kendrick glanced at his best friend and said, "It's cool, gang." He turned to his parents and asked, "What do you want?"

"We decided that now more than ever you need to find a mate and take the throne. Now that your brother is back and shaking shit up, we don't want him to overthrow us," Prima replied quietly, even though everyone in the room could hear her clear as day.

Remington snorted. "You can keep that shit. I don't want the throne. I got what I came for."

His eyes connected with Fallon, and her face flushed under his gaze. She averted her eyes and looked back at Prima and Maximus while Kendrick spoke. "I still don't want the throne."

"You really don't have a choice. All the hard work your mother and I put into the way of life for vampires… we refuse to let it go down the drain or be handed over to another bloodline," Maximus replied.

"Nah…" Kendrick started. "You just want the throne to be given to someone who will allow you two to still get away with whatever you want."

"You think I'll have an issue with doing whatever it is I want, boy?" Maximus asked in challenge. "I can make you find a mate. I think you're forgetting that. I—"

Remington knew what was about to happen, and although he and his brother were at odds, he hated seeing Maximus force anyone to do anything. He looked at his father as a coward, and had no respect for him. He never truly had, and he should be happy Remington even turned him. The only reason he did was because back then, he adored his mother, and he knew she wouldn't truly be happy without his father, even though he was an asshole. Unfortunately, Prima's gift turned her into someone Remington didn't even recognize. In his eyes, she was even worse than his father.

Without even having to think about it, Remington cocked back and punched his father in the back of the head to stop him from uttering a command toward his brother. In the blink of an eye, everyone in the room jumped into action. Scarlette, Axel, and Papa fought off the other members of The Guild, while Remington and his father went toe to toe and Kendrick avoided his mother's touch. Fallon watched in horror at the fight taking place. Prima reached out to touch Kendrick, and Fallon pushed him out of the way, falling victim to Prima's hand instead… but nothing happened.

Prima cocked her eyebrow up and tightened her grip on Fallon before her eyes widened. "Wha—"

Fallon shook her hand off just as Kendrick pushed her aside and faced his mother. "You were going to use your gift on me?"

"To get you to come with us, yes," Prima replied

as she still eyed Fallon with her brows pinched together.

Before either of them could respond, Maximus bellowed, "Enough!"

Everyone stopped what they were doing and looked at him, but Remington smirked as he raised his fist and hit his father once more. "Sorry, Max. Didn't we establish last time that shit doesn't work on me?"

In a flash, Prima was at her husbands side with her hand raised to Remington, and before Fallon understood what was happening, she flicked her wrist. "Stop!"

The entire guild flew up against the walls of The Lair before crashing down to the ground. They were standing seconds later and looking at each other in confusion before looking at Fallon.

One of the vampires from The Guild stepped forward. "A witch."

"Get them," Maximus growled, and under his command, The Guild pressed in on The Fang Gang.

Scarlette quickly turned to Fallon with fear in her eyes and said, "Run, Fallon. Now that they know you're a witch, they will kill you. You need to run."

Remington was at her side as soon as she shook her head, and he tugged on her arm. "She's right, my love. We have to go."

The Guild were now attacking the gang, and Fallon wanted to stay to help, but Remington was tugging at her arm. Kendrick had one of The Guild in a headlock, and he pulled, decapitating the vampire before looking at Fallon. For a moment, she could see the love he held for her there, before he blinked and said, "Go!"

Fallon blinked back tears as she allowed Remington to pull her from the house as he dodged vampires and knocked them out of the way. As soon as they were outside, Fallon got control of her limbs and grabbed Remington's hand. One second she was running with him toward the car, and the next, they were running toward the front door of her grandmother's house. Before Fallon could realize that she just magically transported them on accident, Remington was gone from her side, and she was left at her grandmother's doorstep alone.

THE DOOR WAS SNATCHED OPEN, and Fallon was tugged inside. When the door closed, Lily looked at Fallon and asked, "What's wrong?"

"Where is Remington?" Fallon asked in a panic.

Lily waved her hand dismissively. "He's in the basement tied up. I told you I would think about lowering the defense for you. I didn't say shit about him. Now, tell me what's wrong."

Fallon wrung her hands nervously before expelling a breath. "The Guild showed up at The Lair... where the gang, I mean..." Fallon fumbled with her words because she realized she didn't know how much Lily knew about the vampire world.

"The Fang Gang. It's where they live. I know, chile. What happened?" Lily asked impatiently. It really didn't even surprise Fallon that Lily knew about the gang and where they resided.

"A fight broke out, and you know my powers have always acted on emotion—"

"What happened?" Lily snapped.

"I sort of threw The Guild against the wall telekinetically," Fallon blurted.

Lily walked over to the couch and plopped down with a heavy sigh. "Didn't I tell yo' ass to be discreet?"

Fallon flinched because she felt like a child being scolded by a parent. Those feelings didn't go away just because she had once been the older sister or guardian of Lily. They held each other accountable in any lifetime, and this situation was no different.

Fallon walked over to the couch and sat next to her grandmother. "You know how these things go, Granny. I couldn't help it. Then I accidentally teleported us here… I need help re-focusing my powers so I can get them under control. It's like they've been dormant for so long, and now they're back full-force and going haywire."

Lily eyed her. "You're definitely going to need to get that shit under control because The Guild is going to be gunning for you now. You're an anomaly. There has never been a vampire witch in history. Your powers and strength is going to scare them, Fallon. You're going to need to watch your back. You can stay here as long as you need. My defenses will keep you hidden."

"What about Remington?" Fallon asked, and Lily groaned.

"I forgot about his ass," she grumbled, and Fallon laughed.

"Granny… come on. He's my mate."

She heaved a sigh before pointing a finger at Fallon. "He better not be on no fuck shit, and he better stay out of my way."

"I heard that!" Remington grumbled from downstairs.

Only Fallon could hear him, and she fought the urge to roll her eyes. She could tell keeping her grandmother and Remington from bickering was going to be a task, but what more could she do? She had nowhere else to go, so she stood up and asked, "Can you unbind him, please?"

Lily looked at Fallon like she was crazy. "Girl, why do you keep forgetting you're a witch? That's yo' mate, right? You do it."

With that, Lily disappeared, quite literally, and Fallon heard movement upstairs seconds later and knew her grandmother teleported to her room. Fallon now realized how hard it must have been for Lily to keep her powers to herself while Fallon was growing up.

Shaking her head from those thoughts, she walked down to the basement to free Remington so they could finally have some alone time to talk and get some rest.

Fallon laid in her childhood bed after taking a long hot shower. Remington was lying there already with his phone in his hand, but when she got in bed in his black t-shirt smelling like a Georgia peach, he put it down and gave her his full attention.

"We have to go shopping and get you some clothes," Remington said as he reached over and tugged on one of her ginger curls.

Fallon looked at his toned body. He was only wearing boxers, his pants and undershirt neatly folded and placed on the empty oak dresser in the corner. "We have to get you some, too. I can't believe I accidentally teleported us here. My bags were in the car, but my instincts were to get us out of there quickly. I feel like my magic is all out of whack… but I can feel it. For the first time in over nine hundred years I feel whole."

"That ain't got nothing to do with me?" Remington's crooked smile made Fallon let out an exhausted giggle.

"It has a lot to do with you, too. I can't believe you're here," she whispered, cupping his face in her left hand as she looked into his dark eyes.

He grabbed the hand that was resting on his cheek and kissed it. "Believe it, baby. Nothing could have stopped me from getting to you. I'm just sorry I didn't come sooner."

"Don't be," Fallon whispered. "You came right on time."

When she said that, sadness filled her eyes as she realized Remington had crashed her wedding. She was torn because she had to admit she was slightly relieved she didn't marry Kendrick and make this all even more complicated, but she also mourned for the life she built with Kendrick.

Remington instantly saw the change in her mood, and he took a deep breath. "Look, I know you had to love my brother if you were going to marry the nigga, and I know he loves you. I came here to get you back, no doubt about it, but I ain't in the business of forcing shit. Take all the time you need to get ya mind right, my love, because once you're fully in this, ain't no turning back."

Fallon scooted closer to him and rested her head on his arm. "I am fully in this, Remy. I am sad about

Kendrick, I won't lie, but there ain't shit that can keep me from loving you. You got me. I do need to try to make things right with Kendrick, though. My spirit won't sit right until I do that."

"I feel you. I wish you luck in that shit," Remington replied.

Fallon peered up at him. "You know you could work to make things better between y'all, too, right?"

Remington's jaw clenched. "Nah, man. That ship has been sailed, Fallon. That nigga don't like me, and I don't fuck with his goofy ass, either. It is what it is. I don't need you trying to make peacemaker, either."

"Can't promise that," Fallon replied. "But I need to fix things with him and I first."

They sat in silence for a few moments before Fallon whispered, "How have you really been, Remington? I want to know what you been up to for the last nine hundred years."

He chuckled softly. "That's a lot of ground to cover. Luckily, we have an eternity to talk about it, but to sum it up… I been lonely."

That made Fallon sad. She wished she could love his pain away, but she was smart enough to know that wasn't possible. Remington had to want to heal for himself. She couldn't do it for him. She could, however, support him.

She kissed his chin before saying, "You don't have to worry about that anymore."

He smiled down at her then pulled her in for a kiss. They melted into eachother and seemingly became one. Fallon draped her leg over his side and deepened the kiss when Remington pulled back. "I know what you want, baby, but let's just chill for now."

Fallon looked up at him with wide eyes. "You don't want me?"

He shook his head. "It ain't that, my love. I just want you to fully process what today has brought before you jump into intimacy in that way with me. Less than a week ago you were about to marry my brother. That's deep."

Fallon cringed. She realized him not wanting to have sex had to do with her processing everything just as much as it had to do with him processing the fact that she had been fucking on his brother.

She sighed and pulled away a little before laying her head back on his arm. "I love you, Remington Danger."

"And I love you, Fallon Bordeaux."

Fallon noticed he said it with his eyes closed, and his tone indicated that he needed sleep. "When was the last time you slept?"

"About a week."

Fallon nodded. "Get some rest."

Remington grunted in response, and moments later, he was snoring softly. Fallon chuckled and got comfortable. As tired as she was, she didn't feel the need to sleep. She simply took in the rhythm of Remington's breathing as she pondered the events of the day.

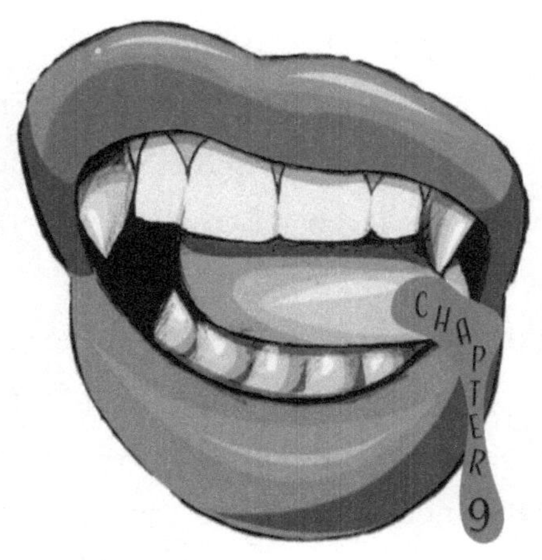

"WHY DIDN'T anyone tell me feeding on blood would make me so horny?" Fallon asked after she wiped her mouth and gently pushed the man aside she had just bitten. He had a look of euphoria on his face as he glanced around her childhood home in a blissful daze.

Remington pulled away from the white woman he had been feeding on and hiked an eyebrow up at Fallon. "Careful, my love. You know I'm the jealous type."

Fallon giggled before asking, "You done?"

He nodded before she grabbed ahold of both humans. She blinked her eyes and found herself a couple of miles away from her grandmother's house. The man looked around in confusion. "Wha—"

Fallon didn't stick around to hear what he was about to say. She took in a deep breath and allowed magic to fill her as she thought of her childhood home. In an instant, she was back in her room, and Remington was standing in the same spot he had been a few seconds ago when she teleported out of the room.

He walked up to her and held her face in his large hand. "You're getting good at that."

Fallon blushed. She had been getting reacquainted with her magic over the past few weeks, and it felt so good. It felt different for her in this lifetime. Stronger and more capable than ever to get out of control. The hardest part about tapping into her magic had been learning to control it, but her grandmother had been there for her every step of the way.

Before Fallon could respond, her grandmother knocked on the door followed by, "I know you just teleported, girl! Bring your behind to the coven room!"

Fallon rolled her eyes playfully.

"I saw that!" Lily shouted from the other side of the door, and Fallon shook her head incredulously.

"It's like she has x-ray vision," Fallon whispered.

"Does she?" Remington asked with his brows raised.

Fallon giggled. "That isn't a power that I know of."

Remington grunted before saying, "You better go

before she does some shit to me because you aren't listening. Put a hex on me or something."

He grumbled the last part, and Fallon barked out a laugh. Her grandmother and Remington bickered a lot, but the two of them thought she didn't see stolen moments where they smiled at each other or cracked jokes. Lily had her guard up, but Remington was definitely chipping away at it little by little.

She reached up and kissed him on the lips, and after a moment, she slipped her tongue into his mouth and moaned. Remington entertained her for a moment before pulling away. "Hot ass. Don't start something you can't finish."

"Who says I can't?" she asked with her eyebrow arched.

He chuckled and pulled away from her, prompting Fallon to let out a low growl with her fangs flashing. His laugh grew louder, and she sighed in frustration. They had yet to have sex, and Fallon had promised herself she would stay patient and wait until the time was right. She understood that a few weeks ago, she had been with Kendrick, so this was more of a respect thing than anything, but she couldn't help her body's natural reaction to want to be with Remington.

He patted her on the ass and said, "Go see what granny good witch wants. I'll be in here... chillin'."

Fallon felt a smile rise on her face because she knew Remington was bored, and that made her happy. If she was being tortured by being around him without being intimate, then he could be tortured by boredom. Fair was fair.

Feeling triumphant, she turned on her heels and dashed out of the room. Aside from re-learning her powers, she was getting the hang of being a vampire. It was never something she wanted, but now that she was, she couldn't imagine it any other way. The speed and strength she had were exhilarating, and both she and Remington suspected she had the gift to block other vampire's gifts. One day, Lily took that theory a step further, and she tested an attack spell on Fallon, but nothing happened. They found that there was a thin line, though. Spells could be cast on Fallon, but not ones that would directly harm her. For instance, she could still be bound and unwillingly transported by magic, but if an attack was used against her, it would simply bounce off as if her skin was made of rubber.

Fallon made it to the coven room and found Lily standing at the huge bay windows looking out them. Without turning around, she said, "What did I tell you about leaving the house?"

"I—"

Lily turned around and glared at Fallon. "You

don't understand that you are being hunted, do you?"

Fallon sighed before falling into a nearby over-stuffed black chair. "I do understand that, but in case you haven't heard, I'm a vampire now, Grandma. I have to feed."

Lily grunted before easing into a chair opposite Fallon and peering at the table across the room that held a spell book and elements of a potion. "And I suppose you aren't going to tell me what you've been working on?"

Fallon shrugged. "I don't think you want to know."

Lily peered at her and shook her head. "Stubborn as hell… as always."

"When do you think my time on lockdown will end? I can't stay here for the rest of my life like a pris-oner, even though I think you are truly enjoying it."

"I am," Lily said, flashing a grin. "Keeping an eye on you is my life's greatest joy."

Fallon huffed out a breath. "Be for real. Has the coven even come up with a plan?"

Fallon had sat in on a few coven meetings, and it was so good to see her coven sisters and get caught up with them via Zoom, but there were a few that didn't want much to do with her because she was now a vampire. It was an odd feeling to be an outcast within her own coven that she helped establish.

"There isn't much to plan, Fallon. The Guild isn't after the coven… they are after you. For all they know, this coven no longer exists. We keep a low profile, so they wouldn't know about us."

"Okay," Fallon drew out. "So it's just fuck me then?"

Lily got up from her chair and walked over to Fallon, pulling her up and embracing her. "It's never just fuck you, chile. There just isn't an immediate threat, especially if you learn to keep a low profile like we do."

Fallon hugged her grandmother back, but she pulled away quickly. "I know this is hard to understand, but I can't do that. The Fang Gang is as much a part of my life now just like the coven is. I don't even know what's happened with the gang and if they're okay… if I could just—"

"No," Lily interjected. Fallon wanted to cry out of frustration. Both her and Remington agreed on one thing… making contact with the gang was out. She didn't have her phone. She realized it must have been lost in the fight back at The Lair, and Remington didn't have any of their numbers. She wanted to do a quick teleport to The Lair to see if she could talk to anyone, but her two bodyguards were making shit hard for her.

Fallon didn't respond. Instead, she walked over to the station where she had been working and picked a vial of liquid up. She jotted its properties down on a notepad and continued working until she felt her grandmother's presence directly behind her. She stopped but kept her back facing her. "Yes?"

"I know you're worried about your friends."

Fallon turned around. "They aren't friends, Grandma. They're family."

Lily nodded. "I understand, but you have to understand you're my family, and I am only trying to protect you. If the shoe was on the other foot, you can't tell me you wouldn't have me locked up in a cage somewhere." Fallon snickered, and Lily continued. "Look… I wasn't even going to do this because I know how you are. I give you a damn inch and you run a mile… but how about this? How about I go out and buy you a new phone so you can at least call them?"

Fallon's eyes lit up before she wrapped her arms around her grandmother. "Thank you."

Lily patted Fallon on the back before asking, "You sure you don't want to tell me what you're working on here?"

Fallon glanced behind her after she pulled away

from the hug then shook her head. Now that she had her powers, she had been working more diligently on the cure for a vampire bite. She was hesitant about telling Lily about it because she knew she wouldn't understand, but she also knew she would have to tell her once the potion was finished. She couldn't allow her or the coven to be blindsided by such a potion. This cure would only allow the creation of more vampires their her minds, but to Fallon, that was not the case. In fact, she was going to make sure to put a cap on it, but it had been something she wanted to get right ever since she got her powers back, and she was close as hell to coming out with a victory.

Lily peered at Fallon with a knowing gaze before she turned around. "I'm going to get your phone and then some groceries for dinner. I'm making red beans and rice and fried chicken with cornbread."

"Sounds good," Fallon replied. One thing she missed about living with her grandmother was her cooking. "And thank you, Grandma. Really."

"Spoiled ass," Lily muttered as she made her way out of the room. Fallon chuckled and turned back to her potion.

. . .

A couple of hours passed of Fallon working before Fallon heard the front door of the house open. A second later, she heard Lily say, "Boy, I got this."

"And so do I," Remington replied smoothly.

She could hear the shuffling of bags before Lily said, "Ass kisser."

"I heard that, Ms. Bordeaux. I ain't kissing nobody's ass but Fa—"

Whap!

"What was that for? You know that didn't hurt, right?"

"Boy, don't tempt me to make something hurt," Lily fussed.

Fallon chuckled but tuned them out as she put the finishing touches on her potion. She smiled triumphantly. Last night had been the game changer for her. There had been a blue moon which only happened every few years. She bound the potion to the blue moon, reciting an incantation before she turned in for the night. That day, she was happy to see the potion settled into a misty blue color. Over the past few hours, she had been reciting incantations and testing a small portion of the potion against human blood properties, and a smile swept across her face after the final test came back in the clear.

"I fucking did it!" she cheered.

"Did what?" Remington asked as he walked into the room with Lily right behind him.

"Language!" Lily snapped.

Fallon ignored her grandmother and said, "I finally completed the cure!"

Remington was in front of her before she could blink her eyes. She giggled when he picked her up and swung her around. He knew how much this meant to Fallon. It was something she had been working on for several years. All she needed was some magic.

"Congrats, baby!" Remington said, placing her on her feet and pecking her on her lips. "That's major. Do you understand how this can change things for vampires worldwide?"

"Cure for what?" Lily asked skeptically as she approached the couple.

Fallon's smile faltered a little bit before she murmured, "Cure for a vampire bite."

Lily's eyes grew wide. "Fallon!"

"Hear me out, Grandma. With a cure like this, we could be saving lives, and I bound it to the blue moon, so only one potion can be produced once every few years. It's not like the goal is to mass produce vampires. It's just here for those who want a mate. It's to fast-track the process and not waste human life."

Lily open and closed her mouth at Fallon's rushed response, trying to figure out what to say. She finally settled on, "You just have it all figured out, don't you?"

Fallon grinned. "And do."

Lily shook her head and tossed Fallon the box that had been in her hands. "Here's your phone."

Fallon's smile widened, and she sat down in the nearest chair so she could set up her phone. While she did, Lily peered over Fallon's notes on the table about the cure. Fallon could hear her grunting every so often, but Fallon had thought this through. She knew Lily was proud of her, even if the stubborn old lady didn't want to admit it.

When she finally had her phone set up and her iCloud contacts loaded, she hurriedly dialed Scarlette's number. Remington took a seat next to her and listened. After a few rings, Scarlette finally answered. "Damnit, Fallon! Where have you been?"

"I—"

"Never mind that! The Guild took Kendrick, Fallon! We've been trying to figure out how to get him back—"

Before Fallon could process what happened, she teleported.

FALLON LANDED right in Scarlette's room. Her best friend was standing at her window, still clutching her phone to her ear when Fallon appeared behind her. Scarlette whirled around, and her eyes grew wide.

"Oh shit," Fallon whispered. "No, no, no."

She knew she was going to be in a world of trouble with both Remington and her grandmother, but she hadn't meant to teleport. Her magic was strongly tied to her emotions, and hearing what her bestie had to say caused her to react... simple as that, but she knew her two bodyguards wouldn't see it that way.

"Fallon... how the fuck—"

"No time," Fallon said before dashing into Papa's room. He was lounging on his bed watching TV when Fallon grabbed his arm and rushed them to Axel's room.

"Hey—"

"Hush," Fallon snapped at Papa as she knocked on Axel's door impatiently.

"What are you—"

Fallon cut her eyes at Papa, and he clamped his mouth shut. Axel finally opened his door, and his brows raised in surprise when he saw Fallon, but she didn't give him a chance to speak. She grabbed his arm and rushed them all back into Scarlett's room.

"Scar, hold on to my arm," Fallon demanded.

"What the hell is—"

"Now," Fallon snapped, cutting her best friend off.

Scarlette quickly did as she was told, and Fallon teleported them back into her grandmother's house, bypassing the defenses completely, so the three vampires she brought with them wouldn't get locked in the basement with their hands bound.

Back in the coven room, Remington and Lily were arguing back and forth about where Fallon had gone, whose fault it was, and how they were going to get her back, but they stopped when Fallon returned with visitors. They stared at her for a few moments before Lily said, "Oh hell no."

"Grandma—"

"Aht!" Lily snapped as she glared at the three vampires she was unfamiliar with.

Papa's smile grew as he took a step forward, bending at the waist and bowing dramatically, his nose damn near touching the ground. "You must be the lovely Lily. Fallon has told us so much about you."

Lily peered at Papa for a moment longer as he straightened up and gave her a dazzling smile before she said, "I like this one. He can stay."

Fallon rolled her eyes as Papa shook her hand triumphantly.

"Not to be rude… it is so nice to meet you, Mrs. Bordeaux, but Fallon," Scarlette said, sweeping her eyes to her best friend. "What the hell was that?"

"And where are we?" Axel asked as he stepped forward, glancing around for a threat and positioning himself in front of his sister.

"I'm sorry, guys," Fallon groaned. "I am still learning to get control of my magic. Its like being a vampire has it all out of whack. It's more powerful now, which means it is more likely to get out of control. When Scarlette told me Kendrick was missing, I accidentally teleported to Scarlett. I knew Remy and Grandma would be worried, and I thought it would be easier to just talk in person… so I teleported you all back here. We are at my grandmother's house, Axel. We're safe, I promise."

He peered at Fallon for a moment before nodding his head curtly, his jaw flexing. She could tell he hadn't had much sleep, even for a vampire, and she felt bad. She opened her mouth to ask a question, but Papa beat her to it. "Fuck all that. Bitch, you can teleport? Ohhhh take us to Paris, Fallon. Wait… it's cold there this time of year… right? Ah, it's just getting cold. It shouldn't be too bad. Paris is the city for love—"

"Boy, hush," Scarlette hissed. "Ain't nobody thinking about love right now. We need to get Kendrick back! He's been gone for weeks! Who knows what they're doing with him over there."

"Weeks? They took him the day I left?" Fallon asked.

"We weren't a match for them niggas, Fallon. We're lucky as hell to be alive," Axel spat.

Fallon nodded, but worry grew in her heart. Had she known Kendrick was in trouble, she would have been taken action. She looked at Lily with pleading eyes, and Lily shook her head subtly before sighing heavily, but before she could speak, Remington did. "I ain't trying to hear whatever you're about to say, Ms. Bordeaux. I might not like the nigga, but I'm siding with Fallon on this one. We have to get my brother back. Nobody deserves to be held captive by The Guild against their will."

"Grandma, please," Fallon pleaded as she walked over to Lily and took her hands in hers.

"Let me call a meeting with the coven. If you are going to do this, I would feel better if we had back up, you hear me? So, just wait so I can figure this shit out. Who ever heard of vampires and witches working together?" she grumbled before shooing everyone from the room. "Gone, get. I have a meeting to call. And you three might as well make yourselves comfortable. Y'all not about to be coming in and out of here, allowing other vampires to find my place of rest. Stay here until all this shit is over with. Now, get out."

Fallon ushered everyone out of the room before Lily slammed the door on them. Papa looked around at the others and placed a hand at his heart. "She is the sweetest old lady I ever met."

Fallon rolled her eyes before leading them down to the kitchen so she and Scarlette could start dinner while they filled her and Remington in on the last few weeks.

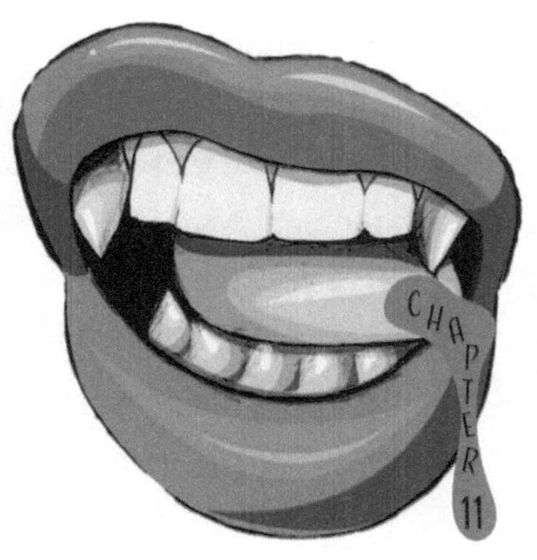

WHY PAPA INSISTED on sleeping in Remington and Fallon's room, Fallon would never understand. She could tell the gang hadn't slept much, though, so she wasn't too upset about it. She let Papa sleep in their bed, and after bickering with him because he thought Fallon and Remington were gong to sleep in the damn bed with him, she was finally free to check in on Scarlette and then Axel, who were sharing the guest room.

All afternoon, they got caught up and ate a hearty dinner. Lily kept to herself for the most part, facilitating the first in person coven meeting in centuries. Fallon had a feeling she was also cornered having so many vampires in her space. Once Fallon checked in on Axel and Scarlette, who were sound asleep, she went to her grandmother's room and knocked.

"Grandma?" Fallon called.

"Come in," Lily responded, and Fallon pushed open the door. Essential oils hit Fallon's nostrils, and she smiled. It was a smell she grew used to as a child. Lily loved burning them. She said it kept her room in a state of peace. Fallon looked around and smiled at the cool tones. The carpet was midnight blue, the walls were deep purple, and the bedspread was gold with navy and purple designs swirled around. Not much had changed in the years Fallon had been gone, and she found comfort in that.

Lily was sitting in the middle of her bed in a sukhasana position, cross legged with her eyes closed.

"Am I interrupting?" Fallon whispered.

Lily opened her eyes and said, "Just finishing up my meditation."

Fallon walked further into the room and sat on the bed next to her grandmother. "Long day?"

Lily sighed "Very. I won't lie, Fallon. I'm having a hard time with all this. Vampires in my house? Lawd… who thought I'd see the day?"

Fallon chuckled. "Grandma, Remington and I have been here for weeks."

She waved Fallon off. "I like y'all, though." As if she realized what she said, her eyes grew wide as she said, "Don't tell Remington's ol' big headed ass I said that."

Fallon heard a faint chuckling from downstairs, and she did her best to hide her grin. The thing about Lily was she could practically read Fallon's mind. Her eyes lifted to the ceiling as she muttered, "I'm going to have to put a soundproof spell on this damn room."

Fallon grabbed Lily's hand. "Thank you."

Lily didn't have to ask Fallon what she was thanking her for. She nodded and said, "I'm not going to let you fight this alone. I knew how much that Kendrick boy meant to you when you chose him over me—"

"It wasn't like that, Grandma. I didn't know," Fallon explained. Had she realized who her grandmother was... who *she* was, she would have fought harder to have them both in her lives. She never would have abandoned Lily like that.

"Hush, chile. I understand the circumstances. Still, I know how much that boy means to you... even if you do have a new mate in the form of a thorn in my ass."

Remington snorted from downstairs, and Fallon bit back her own laugh while Lily continued. "I know there is nothing I can say to make you change your mind and stay out of this... so all I can do is fight with you."

Fallon nodded with tears in her eyes. "I love you, my Lily flower."

Lily's eyes sparkled. It had been centuries since she heard that. It was something Fallon used to say to her in their previous lives.

"I love you too, Fallon."

Fallon stood up and headed toward the door. "I promise once all this is over, you'll have your house back. We all really appreciate you, Grandma."

Lily waved her off. "Having the company isn't so bad. Even if it is a bunch of vampires. This old lady was getting a bit lonely. I especially like that Papa. He's a nice young boy."

Fallon had so much to say about that statement. Papa may have looked young, but he was anything but, and if Lily knew how many humans Papa killed in order to find his mate, she might re-think her statement. Still, Fallon knew Papa had a light. Lily was drawn to that, and she wasn't wrong for it. Papa was the sweetest soul driven to madness in the quest to not feel so lonely. He had his faults, but he really was a good vampire at the end of the day, so Fallon didn't correct her grandmother.

"Why didn't you have any of the coven sisters come live with you?" Fallon asked out of curiosity. In previous lives, the coven was always so tight-knit, and it wasn't uncommon for some of the witches to live together.

Lily shrugged. "Since we are all so far apart, it was natural for everyone to start forming their own family's, much like I had with you and your mother, but she is gone now, and when you left, all the other witches that are living right now were married and doing their own thing."

Fallon bit her bottom lip because there was a question she had been wanting to ask her grandmother for a few weeks now. Lily eyed her and said, "What is it, chile?"

Fallon met her grandmother's eyes and asked, "How did my parents really die? I mean, she was a witch, right? You told me a car accident, but I find that hard to believe."

The subject of her daughter was a touchy one. Tears shone in her eyes as she looked at her granddaughter. "Everly was a first time witch and stubborn as hell. She inherited that trait from you, somehow, even though you are her daughter in this lifetime. Her death is something I want to discuss with you, but it will bring up a lot more questions, and I think we need to focus on the meeting tomorrow."

Fallon wanted to argue, but she realized her grandmother was right. Fallon needed to stay focused so she could rescue Kendrick. The mystery of her parent's death would have to wait.

"Okay, but once this is all over, I want to know everything," Fallon replied.

Lily nodded and said, "Let me get some rest. Tomorrow is going to be a big day."

"Good night," Fallon said before closing the door.

She sighed heavily before making her way down the stairs. Her heart lead her straight into Remington's arms, who was waiting for her in the living room. "How's my baby?"

"Mentally exhausted," she replied.

He chuckled. "Good thing we fed this morning, otherwise you would be physically exhausted, too."

"True shit," Fallon replied before pulling back slightly and gazing up at her mate. "How are you?"

His brows bunched together, and he took his time before responding. "I ain't get the chance to try to save Audrey before I killed her, but I'm getting that chance with Kendrick. Nothing is going to stop me from saving him. My beef with that nigga is deep, but he's still family. Blood. He ain't dying on my watch. It's still fuck him, though."

Fallon giggled. "Let that shit go, Remy."

He grunted in response, and Fallon shifted gears because she knew talking about Kendrick would only end in a difference of opinion. "I don't suppose you're ready to tell me what your gift is, Mr. Danger?"

Remington gave her a crooked smile. "You sure you want to know?"

"Yeah," Fallon breathed as she walked backward since he was pushing her gently toward the wall. She had been trying to gauge his gift for the past few weeks, but she kept coming up empty handed.

When her back touched the wall, he placed his hands above her head and leaned down into her. "I can't die."

Fallon's face twisted up. "What you mean, you can't die?"

"Exactly what I said, love. I can't die. Trust me… I've tried."

Fallon winced at that. "Like… at all?"

"At all," he replied seriously. "Cold doesn't even effect me like it does y'all. It hurts like a bitch, but I can stand it. When my family left me all those years ago, thinking I would die… they were wrong. I stayed for many years in the cold as punishment, but eventually, I left and tried killing myself in other ways, but it can't be done. Finally, I accepted the fact that I'm truly immortal. Not even other vampire's gifts can work on me anymore. They did when I first turned, but everything was stronger back then. The thirst, their powers… all that shit. I'm assuming it died down after awhile because when I came back for you, I realized my mother's touch no longer worked, nor my father's compulsion. From what I can tell, Kendrick can't see me anymore, either."

Fallon blinked up at him slowly. "Impressive."

He chuckled. "I guess."

"Does that mean I'm like you, too?" she wondered. "Their abilities don't seem to work on me, either."

"I thought about that. There is a difference between you and I, though. I'm not immune to spells like you."

"How do you know?"

"When you're in that coven room working, you really tune everything out when you're really in the zone, you know that?" He chuckled.

"What do you mean?" she asked, and she was trying to stay focused on the conversation, but the way he was looking down at her, and the hardness pressed up against her belly button was trying to snatch her attention.

"Granny good witch tried a feel spells on me, and let's just say a few of them hurt like a bitch," he replied.

Fallon gasped, and her attention snapped back up to his eyes from his lips where they had been. "Why would she do that?"

"She was probably trying to see if all vampires were immune to her spells. I think it made her nervous, so she wanted to be sure." He chuckled. "Although, I think she took great pleasure in trying them out."

Fallon peered up at him through he thick eyelashes. "You don't seem so upset about it."

He shrugged. "I'm not. She's cool people as far as I'm concerned. Now, you want to keep talking about granny good witch, or you want to tell me about that shit you was talking earlier after you were done feeding?"

Fallon's body became hot all over as she reached her arms up and clasped her hands behind his neck. "Why talk about it if I can show you?"

"Show me, then," he replied before licking his lips.

"Don't play with me, Remy. You for real?" Fallon asked seriously.

Remington leaned closer to her face. "I can't deny that pussy for an eternity. I think it's been long enough. What you thi—"

Fallon didn't allow him to respond. She kissed him passionately, allowing her tongue to explore the depths of his mouth. After several long moments, Fallon pulled back briefly and whispered, "Invisibilis."

A cooling sensation overtook their bodies and settled around them.

"The fuck was that?" Remington asked.

"I made us invisible," Fallon replied before kissing his chin.

"Can't nobody see me right now?" he asked, and Fallon laughed.

"No, nigga. We are in the middle of my grandmother's living room with a house full of nosy ass vampires. I didn't want anyone coming down here and see us. It only lasts for an hour, so—"

Fallon blinked, and Remington was undressed. She bent over at the waist laughing. When she was through, she straightened up with a smile still playing at her lips and asked, "Thirsty much?"

"I been doing my best to respect your position as well as my ugly ass brother, but I've waited over nine hundred years for this, my love. I'm very thirsty."

Fallon gulped as he walked toward her. "You two look alike."

She wasn't sure why she pointed that out other than to say if he thought Kendrick was ugly, he was, too. Remington stopped walking, his dick leading the way, and cocked his head to the side. "I ain't tryin' to hear all that, Fallon. Do this invisibility spell cover sounds, too, or am I going to have to put yo' face in one of Granny's throw pillows?"

"It covers sound," Fallon stammered.

"Bet," Remington replied as he advanced on her, closing the gap between them. In one swift motion, he pulled her shirt over her head. She wasn't wearing a bra, so her perky breasts were on full display. Next, he tugged her pants off before discarding her panties in a pile on the floor with the rest of her clothes.

In an instant, Fallon was held up against the wall with her legs wrapped around Remington's waist. He kissed her neck, his fangs playfully nipping at her skin. "Fuck I missed you," he groaned.

"I missed you too," Fallon panted, and before he could make another move, she reached down and grabbed his dick. It was long and thick, just like she remembered it, and she moaned involuntarily just at the touch.

"Show me how much you missed me, Fallon," Remington whispered in her ear before biting her lobe. Her back arched, and without wasting another second, she lined his dick up with her opening, and he pushed himself into her.

They each gasped at the contact before Remington went to work. It was Fallon's first time having sex as a vampire, and everything was heightened. The sounds, the sensation, all of it. She could even feel her magic humming through her body, and she prayed she didn't accidentally teleport them somewhere or throw Remington against the wall teleki-netically.

"Ah, Remy… baby!" Fallon squealed as he consistently touched her g-spot with the tip of his dick.

He went harder, moving them around the living room with speed that once would have made Fallon dizzy. Now, her eyes could keep up with everything moving around her, and it was exhilarating. She wasn't the breakable human anymore, and Remington was free to fuck her as roughly as he pleased.

"This your dick?" he asked as he pounded into her. He had maneuvered them so she was bent over the couch, and he was behind her wetting his dick up nicely.

"It better fuckin' be," Fallon groaned as she fucked him back, relishing in the feel of him. For a moment, she felt bad about having sex with Remington at a time like this, but she shook the guilt away as an orgasm built up in her core.

"Tell me this is my pussy, Fallon. I'm about to nut all up in it, baby. Tell me its mine while I fill you up," Remington said through gritted teeth.

"It's yours," Fallon shrieked as her legs shook. A powerful orgasm overtook her, and she rode the wave for a few blissful moments while Remington emptied his seed inside her.

"Fuck," he said as he gently eased out of her.

Fuck was right. It may not have been the longest session, but the excitement at being intimate again caused them to have the most powerful orgasms they'd ever experienced. Fallon was glad her stamina was supernatural now, because almost instantly she was ready to go again. She turned around to face Remington, and he saw the glint in her eye. He chuckled. "Can you do that invisibility shit again?"

Fallon grabbed him by the chin. "I can do it as many times as we need."

"Shit," Remington replied before he dropped down to his knees and lifted one of Fallon's thighs, placing his head right at her center.

Fallon sighed blissfully as she prepared herself for a long ass night.

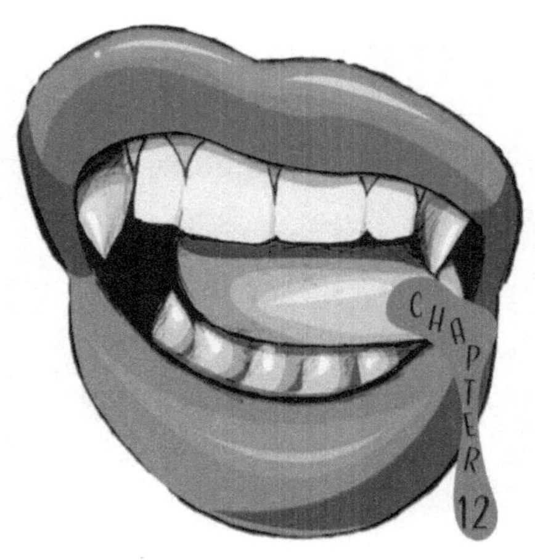

THE NEXT AFTERNOON CAME QUICKLY.

Fallon and Remington spent the night fucking around the living room until the other vamps started waking up. They quickly straightened up, and Fallon removed the invisibility spell just before Scarlette made her way into the living room with tousled hair and morning breath.

One by one, the people in the house woke up and came down to the living room where Fallon and Remington were casually watching TV, as if they had been doing so all night. Lily had been the last one down, and she let everyone know they could fend for themselves for breakfast, but she was making a big lunch. Scarlette jumped at the chance to help Lily in the kitchen, and Fallon was glad. She wanted her grandmother to spend some time with her bestie so she could loosen up a bit.

Fallon thought it worked because by the time her coven sisters started arriving, Scarlette and Lily were setting food out and laughing like old friends, which gave Fallon time to get ready for the day and sit in her excitement about seeing her coven. Both she and Remington had been all smiles, and everyone had been looking at them funny. Papa was finally the one to go ahead ask the question as soon as they all sat down at the elongated table Fallon put a spell on to fit everyone for this luncheon meeting.

"You got some dick, didn't you? You nasty bitch," Papa leaned over and asked.

Both Remington and Scarlette, who were sitting on the other side of Fallon, snickered, and Axel, who was on the other side of Papa stiffened and turned slightly so he was facing away from them. He was always so loyal to Kendrick, and Fallon had to appreciate that about him. She nudged Papa hard in the side, and he yelped before she hissed, "None of your damn business."

"You ain't gotta say it, sis," Scarlette interjected. "Anyone with eyes can see that shit."

A blush overtook Fallon's entire body as Remington pulled her into him by her head and rubbed her soft curls lovingly. He kissed her forehead and whispered, "Ignore them."

She didn't respond because Lily stood from her

seat at the head of the table with tears in her eyes. She wasn't a sappy woman. Never had been, but seeing her coven sisters all in one room really made her beam with joy. Fallon could tell she had missed them, and so had she. The love her sisters poured out to her upon their arrival was overwhelming. She hadn't seen them in centuries, yet the happiness they had for her at getting her powers and memory back was unreal. Some of them were extremely hesitant to hug her and speak with her because she was now a vampire, but Fallon hoped in time they would warm up because she missed the sense of family she remembered having all that time ago. Today was the first step in getting that back.

She sat back and held Remington's hand nervously as she watched her coven sisters. They were all shapes, sizes, and ages. Some were only eighteen, and some were older than Lily. Some came alone because their family members either were not a part of the coven or too young to attend the meeting, and some were families with three generations of witches in attendance. A lot of them had been her own family in past lifetimes, and she had fond memories with almost every one of them, unless they were new witches or had become new witches since she had been gone. In total, Fallon counted twenty-two coven members at the time, which was great. It meant that after all these years, her coven was thriving, and her heart swelled.

"It's so good to see you all." Lily beamed, and the coven responded with positive affirmations. Once the chatter died down, Lily continued. "I only wish it were under better circumstances. As you know, Fallon has her memories back. We aren't sure why they were suppressed in the first place. My best guess is the powers that be felt it was punishment for creating the vampirism potion. It defies the odds of human nature, and magic pulls directly from nature. My theory is the loophole was her turning into a vampire herself, which opened up her third eye to her memories and powers."

Fallon stiffened. She never knew Lily suspected that. As she processed what her grandmother was saying, she realized it made the most sense. Back when she created the vampirism potion, she knew in the back of her mind that it was wrong. She would be creating something that went against the natural order of things, but she did it anyway in the name of love.

There were murmurs around the table, and it seemed as though everyone stopped eating the lunch Scarlette and Lily prepared as they tuned into the conversations around them. Fallon shrunk into Remington while he rubbed her arm reassuringly.

After a few moments, Lily raised her hands, and the chatter died down once again. "That's neither here nor there. Fallon is one of us, but she is also one of *them* now. I'm sure you all remember how hard headed Fallon can be."

There were a few snickers, and once again, Fallon blushed. She hated being ridiculed in this way, but she also felt a sense of comfort because she was amongst family. Nobody in that room meant her harm, so she found a slice of peace in that.

"The Guild has taken one of her own... a vampire. The king and queen's own son, actually, and Fallon is planning to get him back. The reason I asked you here is to see if anyone will help us."

Once again, people started talking all at once, and Fallon picked up snippets from everyone. The tension was high, and Fallon could feel it from every angle. It felt unbearable, and she had to close her eyes and take several deep calming breaths. When she felt a sense of tranquility wash over her, she tuned back in and opened her eyes, only to find everyone sitting calmly, including Lily, who had been standing a moment ago. Everyone had serene looks on their faces, and Fallon's brows furrowed. She looked at Remington, who was looking back at her in confusion.

"What the fuck just happened?" he asked.

Fallon glanced around the table before she put her hand up in front of Papa's face and waved it a few times. He lazily swatted her away and said, "Stop, Fal."

A lazy grin spread on his face, and she turned to Remington in confusion. "I don't know. I took a moment to tune everything out and when I felt calm, I opened my eyes, and everyone was… like this."

She waved her hands around, indicating everyone at the table. Remington looked at her for a few moments longer before looking around the room and saying, "I think you did this, my love."

"Huh?" she asked in bewilderment. "Did what?"

"I've wondered for awhile what your gift might be. I knew it had to be more than being able to block other gifts and certain spells because I can essentially do that as well. You've always considered yourself an empath, right?"

Fallon nodded slowly. "Right… most witches are."

"What if you can control other people's emotions?"

Her eyes grew wide, and she shook her head. "No, I can't—"

"Just try. Whatever you just did, try to reverse it," Remington encouraged.

She looked around the room one last time before

gazing back at him. "I don't know how, Remy. This is ridiculous—"

"Just try," he replied patiently.

Fallon huffed out a heavy breath before closing her eyes. She felt something pulling within her chest, so she focused on that and reeled it in. After a moment, it snapped back to her, and chatter filled the room once again. When Fallon opened her eyes, she noticed everyone looking around in confusion at what just happened. When Fallon met Remington's eyes, he was smiling at her like he had it all figured the fuck out.

"How did you know?" Fallon asked in amazement.

He shrugged his shoulders. "You forget I'm just as in tune with you as you are with me."

Fallon nodded and focused her attention back on Lily, who was speaking again. "I won't hold you all for long. I think that food has us all ready for a nap." There were chuckles surfacing around the room as people looked around nervously. Fallon shrunk down further in her seat, and Lily eyed her for a moment before continuing. "I know Fallon and I are asking a lot of you, but if there is any chance we can get some help, it'll only widen our odds of coming out of this alive. Are there any questions?"

Samiyah, a witch around Fallon's age who with

dark skin and long black hair stood and said, "I have one. Who here has been killed by The Guild before?"

Several hands shot up, and Fallon's heart ached. Samiyah looked around the room and let the weight of that sit with everyone before she looked directly at Lily, and then at Fallon. "My next question is, why should we care about The Guild's son? Fallon, I love you. I have spent many lifetimes with you. We have taken care of each other before in many different roles... but why should we take on this fight?"

Fallon looked her directly in the eye and said, "I don't expect any of you to take on this fight with me. I am more than willing to do it alone, if I have to."

The corners of Samiyah's lips turned up, and she looked at Lily. "Since that's the case, why not turn this into a fight to dismantle The Guild altogether? Fallon is one of us, right? But she is also one of them now... this is an opportunity for us to stop being hunted and live freely once again. We could have all our meetings in person again and come together as a coven should. If we dismantle The Guild as we know it, Fallon could step in and create new order on both sides."

"Woah—"

Fallon was cut off by Axel, who said, "I've been thinking the same thing."

Fallon looked at him with wide eyes, and he shrugged. "It makes the most sense, sis."

"But I—"

"That is an interesting proposition," Candy, one of the older witches cut Fallon off.

Conversations broke out amongst everyone, and Fallon looked at Remington once again. He was looking at her knowingly, and she sighed before asking, "What?"

He shrugged, much like Axel had a moment ago. "I can't say I hadn't thought of it myself."

Her eyes grew wide, and she threw her hands up in disbelief. "Remy, I can't step into a position of leadership. I don't know anything—"

Papa butted in. "Fallon, when you become boss bitch in charge, can you make me your right hand man? I'm trying to elevate my status to show everyone I am that bitch." He snapped his fingers dramatically before sticking out his tongue and twerking a bit in his seat.

Fallon couldn't respond because Lily was calling order once again. When everyone quieted down, she looked at Fallon and asked, "What do you think?"

She sighed and sat back in her chair. "I don't mind dismantling The Guild. They need to be stopped, anyway, and if I can rescue Kendrick while doing so, I'm all for it... but I'm not so sure about being put in a position to lead and bridge the gap between vampires and witches." She turned to Remington and asked, "How do you feel about all this?"

He grabbed her hand and said, "My parents have been dead to me for a long time. I still have a little sympathy for Kendrick, so I want to save him, but to hell with the rest of them. Let them burn."

A few cheers sounded around the room, and someone said, "Oh, I like him."

Fallon cut her eyes at the eighteen year old witch who said it. She was a new witch with amber colored eyes and toffee colored skin. The way she looked at Remington let Fallon know she was hot in the ass and hoping for vampire and witch unity so she could see what the hype was about. Fallon's glare made the young girl slink back into her seat as Remington continued. "After that, I'm with you whatever you decide."

"How about we allow Fallon to think about what she wants to do afterward? For now, those of you willing to help take down The Guild, we have some planning to do. Anyone not willing to help, we understand. This is a lot, and most of you have families and children to think about. You may leave now, and we will keep you informed of everything along the way."

Fallon watched as several witches stood from their seats, most of them older. They said their good-byes and wished them luck before teleporting home. Once everyone that wanted to leave left, there were still thirteen witches seated. Fallon smiled because she felt the odds were in their favor, and Kendrick would be home in no time.

Several hours passed until the house was quiet once again. The witches who were going to help get Kendrick back and dismantle The Guild teleported home to get a good night of rest. They would meet back at Lily's house bright and early, and together, they would teleport to Jamaica to end this shit once and for all.

The vampires were all wide awake and not in need of sleep, so they were in Fallon's room talking about the following day while eating snacks and listening to music.

"I don't care about nothing but getting my boy up out of there," Axel voiced while he rubbed the top of of his sister's head.

Scarlette had a pillow in Axel's lap and was lying

on it with her back on the floor while eating gummy worms. "Don't worry, killa. That's all our priority."

"Agreed," Fallon said, snuggling closer into Remington on the bed. Papa had unsuccessfully tried wiggling his way in between Fallon and Remington, so he was currently lying on the other side of Fallon where he forced her to let him lay on her chest with her arm around him. He was such a big ass baby.

"Let the witches handle killing The Guild, and best of luck to them," Papa said as he popped a Hot Cheeto into his mouth.

Fallon popped him on the head, and he yelped before rubbing it, always the drama queen. "Those are my people too, you know? We aren't going to just let them fight that shit on their own. Saving Kendrick is first, but fucking The Guild up is a heavy second."

"I'm going to make sure my parents are dead. They been taking shit too far lately, and I've given them enough passes," Remington said. "Y'all get Kendrick out of there."

"I'll be right there with you, baby," Fallon said. "Just as soon as I know Kendrick is okay."

His jaw tensed. He knew how much Fallon cared about his brother, and he would be lying if he said that shit didn't hurt a little, but he knew Fallon was locked in and his for an eternity, and that was his peace at the end of the day.

"Y'all are just too cute," Papa said whimsically as he propped himself up so his chin was resting in his hand.

Fallon's eyes grew wide, and she grinned. "Papa! I completely forgot!"

"Forgot what, bitch?" Papa asked.

Fallo didn't respond. She jumped up and dashed out of the room, giggling because she heard Remington chastising Papa for calling her bitch all the time. That shit didn't bother her, though. It was just the type of friendship she and Papa had. She made a mental note to have a talk with Remington about that as she grabbed the vial containing the cure in the coven room and sprinted back upstairs. She hopped on the bed excitedly before tossing Papa the vial. "I finally did it, Pablo!"

"Did what?" he asked as his face scrunched up while he looked at the cure.

Fallon grabbed Papa's free hand and looked him in the eyes. She knew how much this meant to him, and she was so excited for whatever it was he decided to do with the cure. "It's the cure, Papa. Slip this into someone's drink... bite them and drain them, and this will guarantee you will turn them. Now, it doesn't guarantee a romantic mating bond, but—"

"Thank you!" Papa yelped as he tackled Fallon.

They fell onto the mattress, and Fallon could feel Remington's legs under her as Papa kissed her face all over. She giggled wildly until Remington pulled them apart.

Fallon sat up straight, and with a smile still on her face, she said, "Papa, make sure you choose your person wisely. I can only make this cure once every few years. Literally once in a blue moon. Don't just pick the first person you come across—"

Papa waved Fallon off. "Chile, whatever. I'm thinking a fall wedding."

Everyone in the room groaned while Papa chatted on and on to himself about his future with his unknown mate.

FALLON HAD NEVER BEEN to Jamaica. As soon as they teleported, she wished she was visiting under different circumstances. The beach they teleported to had a warm breeze, and the sounds of the waves crashing against the shore enticed Fallon to go for a swim, but she was on a mission, and that didn't include leisurely swimming.

She looked around at her coven sisters as well as the gang before finally looking at Remington. He squeezed her hand before saying, "Don't stray too far from me."

Fallon nudged him in his ribs and said, "Why would I? I'm using you as a shield, Mr. Can't Die."

He barked out a laugh, and his fangs glinted in the bright sun. Fallon clapped her hands together, and everyone looked at her. "Remember, I'm going to try to shift everyone's mood, but you all need to be on the defense just in case. I don't know that I have full understanding of my gift just yet, so I need you all to be ready for whatever. Kill the king and queen first. Hopefully, with them dead, the others will submit, but we will have to be ready for anything." She turned to the gang. "We'll find Kendrick. We don't know what kind of state he will be in, so Papa and Scarlette, you to will be in charge of getting him out of there. Samiyah will come with you to teleport you back to Grandma's house. Axel and I will stay to help the coven, yeah?"

Axel nodded. "As long as Kendrick is safe, I'm all in."

"Cool. Let's go," Fallon said, and everyone turned to look up at the looming mansion built right on the beach. It was far enough away that they couldn't be detected, but close enough that they could make out the black oddity. It was a stark contrast to the beautiful beach it sat on, and it was the only home for miles. Remington had been keeping tabs on his family for years now, so he knew exactly where the mansion was. He didn't know the layout of the inside, though. That part would be a surprise.

Lily cast an invisibility spell on everyone, and as a unit, they trekked toward the mansion. By the time they made it to the stairs leading to the front door, some of the witches were huffing and puffing. Fallon did not miss that. Since turning, she never ran out of breath, and she was thankful for that, especially at that moment.

"Aperta," Fallon whispered, and they could hear a lock clicking, indicating the front door was now unlocked.

Axel pushed his way to the front of the group and eased open the door. When he saw the coast was clear, he waved everyone else in, and they found themselves inside a large foyer with black and white marble floors and dark grey walls. It was dark and ominous, but what Fallon thought was strange was that it was completely empty. All she heard was the faint beating of a heart, telling her a being other than a vampire was somewhere in the house. She always envisioned the mansion where The Guild resided as busy and filled with vampires and humans for feeding. This was not at all what she pictured.

Before she could speak, she heard a soft voice say, "Revelare."

Fallon's eyes grew wide, and before she could reverse the revealing spell, she felt the cooling sensation of the invisibility spell lift. Everyone looked around, and Fallon spotted a young white witch at the top of the spiraling staircase. She looked terrified, but Fallon wanted to curse her ass out because what the fuck did she think she was doing? She wasn't a part of her coven, otherwise she probably would have exiled her for putting them in such danger. Fallon didn't get a chance to do anything, though. Prima walked up behind the witch from the shadows and touched the back of her head. The witch screamed in agony before her body collapsed to the ground. Fallon noted that there was no thudding sound, and she knew it was because there wasn't a bone left in the poor girl's body. Next, Kendrick and Maximus stepped out from the shadows. Maximus laughed menacingly before he clapped Kendrick on the back. Kendrick nudged him off, but Maximus didn't seem to mind as he said, "I forgot how useful Kendrick's power was. He saw you coming from a mile away."

"Kendrick, why the fuck would you tell them? We were coming to save you!" Fallon bellowed in frustration.

Kendrick opened his mouth to reply, but his father said, "Silence!"

Kendrick's mouth immediately clamped shut, and Fallon realized Maximus must have compelled Kendrick to tell him if he foresaw any threat to The Guild. Fallon didn't sit there and wait for shit else to happen. She reached for the tension in her chest and closed her eyes just as she saw dozens of vampires creeping out through a side door out of the corner of her eye. She took a calming breath and released that tension before exhaling with calming thoughts on her mind. She had practiced a few times last night on the gang, and she had been successful. She just needed this shit to work on a bigger scale now.

When she opened her eyes, she saw the vampires closest to her had stopped advancing and were making themselves comfortable on the floor with serene looks on their faces. The issue was, so were The Fang Gang as well as her coven.

"Shit," she cursed under her breath at the same time Prima screamed, "What the fuck are you doing? Kill them!"

Fallon quickly looked at Remington, who was already looking her way. He nodded without there being any words spoken between them, and he got to work on the vampires on the floor. She saw him pull one head off before she turned her head and focused on her coven. She didn't know how to target specific people with her newfound gift, so she started tapping on their shoulders and trying to pull them up. She even went as far as to slap Papa in his face, but he didn't budge.

"Kill them!" Maximus bellowed, and Fallon panicked.

"I'm going to have to pull back on the calming shit," Fallon shouted.

"Go ahead," Remington said as he pulled off yet another head. He pulled a lighter out of his pocket and began the process of setting the bodies he'd already taken care of on fire just as Fallon snapped the calming sensation back into her chest.

Vampires from The Guild were descending on them, and she shouted, "Get up, everyone! They're coming!"

The coven looked around confused, but the gang bounced right up to their feet and got to work. Axel dodged all that and rushed right up the stairs toward Kendrick.

"No!" Fallon called. He was running right into danger… literally. Prima and Maximus Danger stood there guarding Kendrick with a few of their most trusted lieutenants. She looked around her, and spells were flying, heads were rolling, and people were dropping like flies. She weaved through all that and raced up the stairs just before Prima raced toward Axel with her palm outstretched.

"No!" Falloon shouted again, and she accidentally pushed a panicked feeling out toward the others. Prima stopped an inch from Axel, and she dropped to her knees grasping at her chest. Axel, Kendrick, Maximus, and the few other vampires in the vicinity did the same, and Fallon looked at them in confusion before she realized they were each having panic attacks. Panic attacks she accidentally pushed out to them, but it worked in her favor. She grabbed Maximus and Kendrick before teleporting back to her grandmother's house. In a blink, they were in Lily's kitchen, and Kendrick and Axel were able to breathe easier, the panic in their chests subsiding. Before either of them could say anything, Fallon looked at Axel and said, "Stay here with him."

"But I—"

"There's no time, Axel, and someone needs to be here to watch him," Fallon said before she teleported back to the massacre happening at The Guild's mansion.

As soon as she appeared, a vampire from The Guild charged her. She threw a punch that sent him flying, and Remington appeared at her side immediately. "That's no good, love. You need to pull their heads off."

"But—"

He shoved a lighter into her hand. "I'll handle that part. You light any headless bodies you see on fire. I'll watch your back."

Fallon nodded, and her and Remington moved through the crowd.

"Ligare!" Fallon shouted, and several vampires advancing on them fell to the ground, bound by invisible rope.

Remington looked at her in appreciation. "This makes shit easier."

She watched as he pulled the first vampire's head off, and just as she was about to light the body, she saw Lily out of the corner of her eye. Her attention was completely snatched from what she and Remington were doing as she watched in horror. Maximus appeared behind Lily and whispered, "Kill yourself."

Lily's eyes grew wide as she turned around to face him. He held a dagger out to her, and Fallon ran as fast as she could toward her grandmother, but Prima intercepted her and punched her so hard, she flew across the room and slid down the wall. Landing on her feet was like second nature to her, and although her jaw ached slightly from where Prima punched her, it was nothing compared to the ache she felt when she witnessed Lily stab herself repeatedly with the dagger.

"No!" Fallon cried as she dashed over to her grandmother, this time uninterrupted. She fell to her knees as Maximus and Prima stood over her chuckling wickedly. Remington appeared, and the three of them started throwing hands like they weren't family, but Fallon didn't pay attention to any of that shit as tears clouded her vision. Normally, death for a witch was more of a celebration because it was a passing into a new time for them, and rebirth was almost always guaranteed, but Fallon and Lily had just reunited, it felt like, so this death hit her a little harder.

"Wake up, my Lily flower," Fallon cried as she watched her grandmother's chest rise and fall one last time. "No!"

Fallon looked around the room with teary eyes, and she saw death right before her eyes. Vampires and witches alike were strewn across the floor, and more were getting injured as the fight continued. This shit could have been so much easier if The Guild hadn't been warned of their arrival. They fucked up royally when they forgot about Kendrick's gift, and it cost not only Lily's life, but many more.

Her eyes dropped back down to Lily, and a heart-wrenching cry bellowed out of Fallon. "Ah!"

When she opened her eyes back up, everyone was crashing against the walls again, and a fire ignited right in the middle of the room, a few feet away from her. With tear-filled eyes, she called to the remaining witches, "Retreat!"

She watched as they did as they were told, a few of the witches grabbing members of TFG before disappearing. Remington was at her side in an instant, crouching down and touching her shoulder. Fallon didn't even wait for him to speak. She teleported back to her grandmother's house, the last thing she saw was Prima and Maximus' angry expressions as they advanced toward her. Luckily, that was a fight she didn't have to partake in that day. She safely landed in her grandmother's kitchen where everyone else was now gathered and tending to their wounds. They stopped when they saw Lily's body, which was now lying on the kitchen counter. Silence filled the room as everyone processed that their coven leader was now dead.

Remington placed a hand around Fallon's waist, but she shook him off. No words were spoken as she looked at Candy, who was a healer. Candy already knew what Fallon was going to ask, and she shook her head subtly. "She's gone, baby. You know healing only works if there is life left in the body."

Fallon nodded once before turning on her heels and walking out of the room. A war had been brewing for centuries with the vampires on the winning end, but shit was about to change. Fallon had a sole purpose moving into the future. Kill Maximus and Prima, and take the throne.

To be continued…

CYN'S CATALOG

Get signed copies at: Cynful Monarch

SERIES:

The Urban Fairytales Series (Complete Collection - all books in 1): https://amzn.to/2V7rk6d

Dust to Diamonds (Book 1 of the Urban Fairytale Series): https://amzn.to/3rT9srt

The Baddest of Them All (Book 2 of the Urban Fairytale Series): https://amzn.to/3lnnSyU

Lil Red Ryder (Book 3 of the Urban Fairytale Series): https://amzn.to/3xoLbKV

Rebel & Her Beast (Book 4 of the Urban Fairytale Series): https://amzn.to/3ih5kyr

A Fairytale Wedding (Book 5 of the Urban Fairytale Series): https://amzn.to/3rQ6O63

The Princess & the Goon (Spin-off of the Urban Fairytale Series): https://amzn.to/3fkDmQf

Billion Dollar Baddie: https://amzn.to/37cGVnr

Billion Dollar Baddie 2: https://amzn.to/3A4GRCm

Anything for the Family: https://amzn.to/3CcdvEi

Anything for the Family 2: https://amzn.to/3w0oqyt

Lux Rose: https://amzn.to/3wuib6e

Lux Rose 2: https://amzn.to/3MrZlCJ

Lux Rose 3: https://amzn.to/3Roq9re

Fang Gang: https://amzn.to/3C6PYFn

STANDALONES:

Baby, it's Cold Outside: https://amzn.to/2V7ZSoX

The Married Woman: https://amzn.to/33k9jp1

A Hood Chick's Savior: https://amzn.to/3ykaAHf

Hell Hath No Fury: Beaten at your Own Game: https://amzn.to/3FmZRyE

COLLABS:

Bosses Link Up: https://amzn.to/37d2292

Endlessly Mine: https://amzn.to/3n0bwfk

<u>VELLA STORIES:</u>

A Hood Chick's Outlaw: https://amzn.to/3rNjdYh

LET'S CONNECT!

Join my readers group on Facebook, and stay up on
all releases, get character visuals and sneak peeks,
and even get in on giveaways!
https://www.facebook.com/groups/
277463019954112/

Hey There!

Thank you for your support on my literary journey. I hope your reading experience was a pleasant one. Please leave a review on Goodreads and Amazon. Please feel free to connect with me to stay current on upcoming releases and reader specific exclusives.

Cyn Alexander